GAY SWEET HOLIDAY ROMANCE COLLECTION

CONNOR WHITELEY

No part of this book may be reproduced in any form or by any electronic or mechanical means. Including information storage, and retrieval systems, without written permission from the author except for the use of brief quotations in a book review.

This book is NOT legal, professional, medical, financial or any type of official advice.

Any questions about the book, rights licensing, or to contact the author, please email connorwhiteley@connorwhiteley.net

Copyright © 2023 CONNOR WHITELEY

All rights reserved.

DEDICATION

Thank you to all my readers without you I couldn't do what I love.

AUTHOR OF ENGLISH GAY SWEET CONTEMPORARY ROMANCE SERIES

CONNOR WHITELEY

LOVE IN THE INGREDIENTS

A CHRISTMAS GAY SWEET CONTEMPORARY ROMANCE SHORT STORY

LOVE IN THE INGREDIENTS

Running his fingers gently over the smooth marble worktop of his kitchen, Sean took a deep breath of the cinnamon scented air, that reminded him of delicious apple pies as a kid, as he prepared himself for his next batch of cookies.

He was never normally this nervous about baking, he loved it, he loved the chemistry and the changes within the baked goods as they cooked and transformed into stunning perfection. But after the year him and his family had had, he just needed everything to go right.

As he felt the warmth from his black oven travel up his legs, he knew he had to get going on the next batch.

Looking at the silver bowl, teaspoons and spices in front of him, Sean sighed a little as he remembered why he was doing all of this. A part of him didn't want to bake yet another batch of cookies, he was sure if this was a normal time, then Sean knew he would have loved to bake even more.

But these were not normal times. At least not to him.

After his parents finding out he was gay in the January and all the loud moaning, screaming and unfriendliness that followed. Sean just wanted his dinner at Christmas to go well, his parents said they were sorry but he just wanted things to be okay.

Sean could hardly say that he wasn't surprised when his mum called up and asked if they could come round today for dinner.

At first Sean so badly wanted to say no, after everything they had put him through, Sean didn't want to see them. But he did love them, care about them and want to see them. So to his utter surprise he said yes.

The sound of cookies sizzling, cars driving past and the quiet Christmas songs in the background made Sean smile and push all those negative thoughts aside. This was going to be great, his parents and him were going to have an amazing dinner. But first he needed to make something special to go with coffee after dinner.

Even that memory of having coffee and something special after a grand meal made Sean relax a little, those times with his posh family were long gone (he wasn't invited anymore) but whilst the time lasted, it was great.

Returning his attention to the neatly arranged bowls, teaspoons and spices in front of him, Sean took out his phone and looked at the recipe.

It was a recipe for Brandy Snaps that one of his friends had sent him, Sean wasn't exactly sure if they were nice or if they were suitable for his parents' posh taste. They sounded posh but in Sean's experience that meant very, very little.

As he looked at the phone and the stupidly small text, Sean read that he needed butter, flour and sugar so he measured it and weight it all out.

With his strong arms mixing the butter and sugar together into a smooth paste before he added the flour, Sean knew this was going to be good. It was butter and sugar, what else did the dessert need?

For a moment, Sean remembered how his sister had actually had that in a sandwich before. Even now Sean hated the idea and found it completely disgusting, but he did love his sister. She was always a laugh. (At least from what Sean remembered)

After mixing that all together, Sean added the vanilla, milk and coffee. He mixed it all up for a few seconds and licked his lips.

Sean knew that if his parents didn't enjoy this then something was very wrong with them. They loved coffee, sweet things and vanilla. This was going to be the perfect thing to finish up a wonderful evening.

A part of Sean wondered if that last part was true, after everything that had happened, he didn't want tonight to be awkward or strange. He had a feeling (knew for a fact) that his father didn't want to come, it was just how he was. It was probably his mum that had arranged it all.

At least he might have one ally in case things go wrong. Sean relaxed a little at that idea, it was silly to feel like he needed allies but after the past year, very little surprised him anymore.

Returning his attention to his phone, he accidentally clicked off the recipe, so as he was trying to find it again. Sean wondered if he would be invited back to family events anytime soon. He wasn't really sure he cared that much, he was fine with being gay and he was more than happy.

It was everyone else that was the problem.

Sean smiled as he thought about the look on his family's face if he bought a boy back to them. Then he frowned as Sean remembered he had never had a boyfriend, he had always been too scared to get one. That needed to change.

After finding the recipe again, Sean looked at the last ingredient that he needed and rolled his eyes. He needed cream.

He didn't have any.

Taking a step away from the bowl of all the delicious ingredients and breathing in the coffee scented air, Sean wondered what to do next. He had to make these brandy snaps for his parents, he couldn't not make them, the fate of his relationship could be on the line.

Forcing himself to relax, Sean looked at the time and frowned when he saw it was four in the afternoon. His parents said they were coming at six, which in real life meant they were coming at half five. Sean didn't have time for this, but he had to make them. He had to find some cream.

As Sean remembered there was a shop within walking distance, he turned off the oven and put his mix in the fridge.

Then he dashed off, not knowing what he was going to find.

***

Hayden stared at his watch as he lent on the cold plastic till with sweets and scratch cards all around him as he waited for customers that were never going to turn up.

The cold air smelt of cigarette smoke from the awful smokers outside and Hayden hated the taste it formed in his mouth. But the sound of the smokers outside, the singing of Christmas Songs and the jolliness of little children running with their parents made him smile for a moment.

Then Hayden turned his attention back to his little shop with rows upon rows of food of all different types for people to buy.

It wasn't even his shop, it was his father's. A part of Hayden wondered why he bothered manning the shop for his father when his father could hire another young person who needed the money (and might actually enjoy it). During the week, Hayden loved being an office worker for his friend's company in insurance. But this customer-less shop was not what

Hayden wanted to do with his Saturday afternoon.

Looking back at his watch, Hayden rolled his eyes as it was only ten past 4, he wanted it to be five o'clock so he could go home and start decorating his Christmas tree in his little apartment.

He knew it would be more fun to have a boyfriend or someone else help him, but Hayden didn't have anyone yet. Normally his best friend came over and they would make a thing out of it, but she was away on business this weekend.

As Hayden listened to the smokers and everyone else walk away from outside the shop, he cocked his head as he wondered if he should just close up early. His father wouldn't mind and if he moaned about loss of earnings (which his father didn't need either), Hayden supposed he could give him some money.

Nodding to himself, Hayden was about to walk out from behind the counter when… wow! (Hayden almost swore)

Hayden's mouth dropped open when he saw an utterly stunning man about his age walk into the shop. The man's hair was beautifully long that seemed to flow down his shoulders like it was made from water.

This Man was fit with strong arm muscles and wearing his tight black coat and black jeans made him look even more stunning.

Hayden couldn't believe how amazing The Man looked. Somehow this Man even managed to make his skin look smooth, young and utterly amazing. But what really did it for Hayden was the Man's striking blue eyes.

The Man was perfection.

Hayden had to stop his thoughts from wondering what he would like to do to the Man's hair and his amazing body.

By this point, Hayden hadn't realised The Man had walked over to the till area with an equally massive smile. Hayden wanted to force himself to say something but he couldn't The Man was so beautiful and that's all he could focus on.

It was that moment Hayden knew he was going to be in trouble (or maybe love).

***

Breathing in the horrible smoke from the smokers standing outside the shop, Sean waved at them as they started to sing Christmas songs at him. But Sean couldn't really understand the image of Christmas singers smoking, the two didn't seem to connect in his mind.

With Sean knowing he had to get some cream no matter what, he watched the smokers put out their cigarettes and walk down the street singing their Christmas songs loudly and he entered the shop.

When he walked into the shop, Sean ignored the rows upon rows of great looking foods and all the other essentials that people would need and didn't want to go to a supermarket for. Instead Sean knew it was best to just ask the person at the till.

As he looked around for the till, Sean felt the cold wrap around him and he was instantly glad he hadn't done what he normally did, and take off his coat as soon as he walked in anywhere.

For a few moments of looking, Sean found the till and the amazing smell of strong aftershave filled the air as Sean looked at the-

Sean didn't know what to think or say or do as he stared into the drop-dead gorgeous eyes of the guy at the till. He was definitely Sean's age with an amazing slim body and short blond hair.

But what really, really, really did it for Sean was the guy's face. It was squarish but it was perfectly smooth and it was perfectly framed by his eyes and hairs with a strong jawline.

The Guy looked like some sort of movie star, he shouldn't have been working in some shop. He should be working on film sets, sweeping up women (and hopefully men) and enjoying being a movie star.

Sean instantly felt bad as he never ever acted like this, whenever he normally saw a guy he liked. He would try and ignore his feelings or he would just suppress them and never act on them. Actually being attracted and thinking like this towards the Till Guy was strange.

But it felt so good to him.

Remembering why he was there (and trying to stop his wayward parts from doing things), Sean walked up to the Till Guy. Partly because he needed cream, partly because Sean had to talk to Till Guy.

But when he got to the till, Sean couldn't stop smiling as he breathed in more of the Till Guy's stunning aftershave and looked deeper into his amazing eyes.

Sean knew he had to talk so he just went for it.

"I need cream. Parents hate me. I'm gay. I need to create a nice dish. They're coming tonight. I need cream!"

As soon as he finished Sean wanted to run out of the shop and never return, but to his (utter) surprise the Till Guy smiled even more and looked to take a few deep breaths.

Sean took a few deep breaths of his own.

"I'm sorry about I know I must have sounded strange. Do you have any cream please?" Sean asked.

"Yes it's in the back next to the milk. And if it helps, it's okay. I don't know about family not taking it well, but I do understand it," the Till Guy said.

For some reason, Sean relaxed and felt a weight he didn't even know he was holding. He had always thought he was okay with what had happened, but he supposed it was nice to hear he wasn't alone in people not liking him.

"Friends?" Sean asked.

The Till Guy nodded.

"I'm sorry to hear that. I'm Sean,"

Sean's eyes narrowed on the Till Guy as he seemed to smile and bite his lip at hearing his name. He wasn't exactly sure how to act, Sean had never had this happen to him before.

"I'm Hayden," Till Guy said.

Now Sean wanted to kick himself as he noticed

he had bit his own lip. Hayden was a hot name. Hell, Hayden was hot!

In some bad attempt to stop himself from doing something foolish, Sean walked to the back of the shop and grabbed a large cold bottle of cream.

"Why are your parents coming tonight?" Hayden asked.

Sean opened his mouth, but he realised he really didn't know.

"I'm sorry. That was probably too personal," Hayden said.

"No it's fine. I just don't know. I just… want it to go well," Sean said, feeling a bit light-headed as Hayden smiled at him once more.

"Have you got a friend going with you?" Hayden asked.

Sean's eyebrows rose. He had no idea why he needed to have a friend, he had hoped everything would be fine without anyone else, but what if Hayden knew something Sean didn't?

"Sorry. I remember when some of my friends wanted to come back. I felt like it helped me to have my bestie with me," Hayden said.

Sean's eyes narrowed. It wasn't a bad idea and he had thought about having allies earlier, maybe this would be a good idea. But who could he call this late on a Saturday afternoon?

Sean wondered what his best friend was doing but he was probably busy with his own boyfriend, his other friends probably had Christmas plans this weekend and… he didn't have anyone else.

The amazing smell of Hayden's strong aftershave made Sean smile as he decided he had to do something crazy.

"Do you want to come?" Sean quickly asked.

As soon as he said it, he felt like an idiot, he had only just met Hayden and he was basically asking him out on a date. He couldn't do that, could he?

Sean just wanted to run out the shop.

But to his surprise, Hayden looked a little flushed.

"Yes," Hayden said, sounding as unsure as Sean.

Sean didn't exactly know what to do so he smiled and pretended to act natural (and completely trying not to panic inside!).

"Great, parents coming at half five. Dinner for six," Sean said failing to sound cool.

Then Sean saw the time on Hayden's watch and his eyes widened. It was half four. He had to go.

He got out his wallet but Hayden touched his hand softly. Sean couldn't help but smile at the pure power flowing between them. he loved it. He loved the feeling. He wanted more.

"Sean, it's fine. I'll pay,"

Sean nodded and gave Hayden a boyish grin as he left the shop, looking forward to dinner for an entirely new reason now.

***

As he watched the shop door close, Hayden's eyes widened as he just realised what he'd done.

Breathing in the cold air with hints of smoke from those smokers earlier, Hayden looked around at all the rows upon rows of food and other essentials. He didn't know what he was looking for but he hoped to find something.

In all honesty, Hayden guessed he was probably looking for a nice bottle of wine or something to take to his new dinner host.

The sound of Christmas songs and cars driving past quietly filled the air as Hayden slowly walked past the shelves of food to the back of the shop where the wine was kept.

A part of Hayden wanted to kick himself for what he just agreed to. Whenever he was normally around boys he was calm, collective and he would never ever agree to go on a random dinner date with a hot man he only just met.

But Sean was special.

Hayden rolled his eyes as he knew he sounded like some loved up person, but he really believed it. He loved Sean's amazing long hair, eyes and his stunning strong arms.

It still didn't make Hayden feel any better, he still felt like he was intruding in something important and something that was nothing to do with him.

But it was.

As Hayden remembered how much support his best friend had given him during his own dinner with friends that had called him awful things. Hayden didn't want to tell Sean that it would be awkward at times and maybe it would go badly.

Then Hayden remembered that it was his best friend that had supported him and made sure it went smoothly as possible. Hayden had always loved his best friend for that.

Yet Sean didn't have anyone like that available.

When he got to the end of the shop, Hayden stared at all the black, clear and even red bottles of wine that were neatly arranged in tall rows on the shelf in front of him. The fridge behind the shelf hummed along to itself and Hayden ran his fingers across the cold glass of the bottles.

Hayden felt his hand shake a little as he looked over and over the wine labels as if his life depended on choosing the right bottle for the dinner. He knew he was being silly but he supposed he wanted, no needed this to go right. He needed Sean to like him but most of all Hayden needed to be there to support Sean.

When his fingers were starting to turn a little numb from the cold glass of all the wine, Hayden touch the label of an expensive red wine from France. It was one of the more expensive ones in the shop but for some reason it felt right.

Hayden looked at the price tag and he surprised even himself. The wine was definitely way over £10, a price he would never consider buying before, but on this occasion it felt right. It felt okay. It felt... good.

Picking up the cold bottle of red wine, Hayden looked around the shop and saw it was completely empty like it was before. There was no one coming, no more customers, no more money coming in today.

Everyone was out living their lives.

So Hayden knew he had to do the same, he had to pay for the cream and wine, go home, get changed and go and support an utterly stunning man.

***

After whipping up the cream with vanilla and sugar added to it, Sean took a deep breath of the stew scented air with other hints of sweet desserts mixed into it too. Sean loved the smell, it was so welcoming, so inviting, so relaxing.

The last one might have been wishful thinking but Sean hoped not. He really, really wanted this all to go perfectly.

As he popped the cream in the fridge for later, Sean pressed his back against the cold grey fridge and took a few more deep breaths. He wasn't relaxed, he knew that but he didn't know why.

He knew tonight was tense and it could go wrong in a million different ways, but Sean knew he was okay on that front. He had made amazing food, even got his parents a present or two each and he had… he had a support person.

Just the reminder of what he had dragged Hayden into made Sean accidentally bang the back of his head against the bridge.

A part of Sean didn't know why he invited a complete stranger into his life like that and more importantly to a dinner with his parents. He supposed he didn't need another factor to annoy his parents. What if his parents didn't like Hayden?

Why did it matter?

Sean cocked his head as he remembered that question from his best friend soon after his parents had said awful things to him. He didn't know why it mattered, but it did. Sean loved his parents, he wanted them in his life, he wanted to be accepted.

But then Sean realised no matter what happened tonight, if Hayden turned up then everything was going to be okay. Hayden was a super hot guy that Sean wanted, needed to be with. Hayden was hot, kind and Sean knew he would be perfect boyfriend material.

Then his stomach churned as Sean wondered what if he was the problem. Sean had never had a boyfriend before, he didn't know what to do, how to date, he-

The sound of a knock on the door made Sean tense then relax as he looked at the time and it was before half five.

It was Hayden. He had actually come.

Sean felt his hands go sweaty as he realised that Hayden actually cared about him. Sean had never known a man to care about him before. Maybe this could work out, maybe tonight was going to be great, maybe-

The sound of the door knocking got louder and Sean smiled as he walked through his house to the door and opened it.

His smile deepened as he looked into the striking blue eyes and stunning movie star face of Hayden. Sean placed his hand on the doorframe and couldn't help but stare at the stunning man in front of him.

Hayden placed his hand on the doorframe too and they both smiled like schoolboys as their fingers touched each other. And it was then that Sean changed his mind about the entire evening, he really didn't care about what happened, because he had Hayden and he hoped that this was going to last a very long time.

And this all happened because of some ingredients.

PARTY, LOVE, CHRISTMAS

With the quiet stand mixer humming and mixing in the background and the sound of the quiet Christmas songs playing too, Percy stared wide eyed at all the streaks of cake batter, sprinkles and flour everywhere. Percy just stared at the beautiful mess in the kitchen. He wasn't sure why he thought it was beautiful, but Percy hoped this mess was going to lead to something magical.

As he stared at the beautiful mess, he shook his head as he breathed in the heavenly scent of the sponges baking in the oven, already for him and his best friend Megan to decorate and assemble for the Christmas party tonight.

Percy could already taste the amazing vanilla and chocolate sponge in his mouth, it was going to be amazing. At least all the baking stopped Percy from worrying for a few moments about the party.

The party wasn't anything grand, it was a normal Christmas party with all the friends and colleagues from his new job in Megan's office. But that didn't make Percy feel any better, he had barely been there a week, and now he had to go to a party!

Trying to push those thoughts away, Percy returned his attention to the messy kitchen and he went to grab a tea towel to wipe it up before he heard light footsteps and Megan, who wore her normal black jeans, loose blue shirt and tennis shoes, pop back into the kitchen.

With Megan slipping past him and returning to her work in the kitchen like there was no mess at all, Percy shook his head and looked at her. Wondering how long it would take her to notice the mess was there.

Granted knowing Megan, she would probably say it wasn't a mess but a part of the baking experience. Percy didn't have the heart to tell her, it was the part of the baking experience *with her*.

As much as Percy loved to cook, create things and give them to people as gifts. He never got this messy and as he took a step towards Megan, he felt flour and wet cake batter under his feet.

"Come on Pers," Megan said. "Need that recipe,"

He had no idea what there was left to make, they had already made sponges, sandwiches and Swiss rolls for the Christmas party. Percy didn't think they needed anymore but Megan always wanted to make her famous (only to her) mini-Christmas puddings, and Percy had learnt a long time ago never to upset

Megan.

As he got out his large black phone and flickered through it, Percy remembered how he had watched plenty of (hot) men go against Megan's wishes before and that never went down well.

Percy never understood why Megan was so stubborn but he had learnt to live and even love it a little.

"Come on Pers! They're waiting for my famous Christmas Puddings!" Megan shouted.

Percy smiled. "Yea, yea,"

After a few more moments of looking, he found the recipe she had sent him.

"Found it Meg,"

"Good. Read out the ingredients to me,"

"Including weights?"

"Heavens no Pers. My famous recipe is wonderful, I've made it so many times. I know it like the back of my hands,"

Again Percy didn't have the heart to tell her that her Christmas Puddings were not wonderful. He almost laughed as he remembered all the times him and his friends had had to secretly bin the puddings.

"Your basic mix, treacle and brandy," Percy said.

For a moment, Percy wondered what she meant by basic mix but when he saw her add flour, butter and sugar to the large silver mixing bowl, he understood. He just hoped these tasted good.

"Know who's coming tonight?" Megan asked.

"Of course not. I only know the people from

HR. They don't go to parties!" Percy said, remembering how depressing his first two days were in HR. He had no idea how much paperwork and health and safety training was involved in his job.

"True," Megan said sounding like she was trying not to laugh.

"Who's going then?"

Megan clicked her fingers and Percy looked back at his phone.

"You need cinnamon, cloves, brandy and golden syrup," Percy said. Maybe these would be good with a bit of golden syrup in them.

"These will be the best puddings ever. Far better than Missy's puddings,"

Percy raised his hand to his forehead as he now understood why Megan wanted to go to the party for the first time. In all the past five years Megan had worked there, Percy had never heard of her wanting to go, most weekends' before Christmas him and Megan finished the Christmas shopping, bought presents for each other and their boyfriends and occasionally went out for dinner.

But now Percy was starting to get why she *had* to go this year.

"Who's Missy?" Percy asked.

Megan turned towards Percy. "You know Pers. That woman who flirts with the boss and gets to leave an hour before me!"

Percy shrugged.

"Stick woman!"

Percy shook his head smiling. He loved the nicknames she gave her friends, peers and basically everyone she met. Percy didn't want to know his.

"There's plenty of boys for you tonight," Megan said. Quickly turning back to the mixture.

Percy looked at her. "Is that what this is about? You want me to hook up with someone,"

"No," Megan said unconvincingly.

"I don't-"

"Pers I love you, but you don't have a boyfriend. You haven't had one for ages and this Christmas party is perfect for meeting new people. Even if you don't meet a boyfriend or hook up, at least try and meet some new people,"

Percy shook his head and knew she was right, he did need to meet some new people and get to know his work friends better.

"Fine,"

"Brillant. Now pass me the salt please,"

As he passed Megan the salt to apparently add a contrast to all the sugar, Percy didn't know whether he was going to find new friends, or save everyone from these puddings!

***

Patrick loved Christmas parties. They were the best things ever to be invented. Even tonight the Christmas songs were playing loudly in the large open plan office and everyone was having fun.

Pressing his strong muscular back against the cold wall of the office, Patrick looked out over the large office that was now a dance floor with men and women of all different ages and sizes dancing along to whatever song was blasting itself.

At the moment it was *Santa Claus Is Coming To Town*, Patrick loved this song but he loved all of the songs, he just loved Christmas. It was such a magical time of year that was full of amazing people, presents and miracles.

Of course it was better to share it with someone but Patrick knew he would find someone eventually. A small part of him hoped he would find someone tonight, he did believe in Christmas miracles after all, but he was going to enjoy the party no matter what.

The smell of all the cakes, sandwiches, sausage rolls and the rest of the things that people bought in a hurry at the local shop before coming to the party.

Patrick had almost forgotten himself that he needed to bring food and some drink for the party so he quickly dashed into a Marks & Spencers and bought a few things without looking. (He knew he'd regret it when he checked his bank account tomorrow!)

With the smell of the amazing food washing over the room, in addition to all the other hints and scents from people's perfumes and aftershaves, Patrick couldn't stop smiling as he soaked in all the amazing vibes of the party.

There wasn't a single person frowning or being sad. Everyone was happy, alive and partying. Even the people from HR were dancing!

If that didn't confirm Christmas miracles were real, then nothing would.

As the song changed to *Santa Baby*, Patrick checked his expensive gold watch and wondered when Megan was going to turn up. Patrick didn't want to see her famous (famous for the wrong reasons) Christmas Puddings, but he did want to see her. She was always a laugh and fun to be around.

Megan had said that she was bringing a friend that Patrick would like to the party, but from past experience, Patrick knew that meant very little. Megan was friends with the best people on the planet to some of the less good people and everyone in between.

For all Patrick knew this friend would be a paper pusher for the government or a fireman. Patrick smiled at the last idea, he definitely wouldn't mind Megan bringing a fireman to the party.

Noticing there was a little less dancing, Patrick returned his attention to the middle of the office and saw some people were opening the massive glass doors to let two people walk in.

Patrick instantly smiled when he saw Megan in her long black dress and holding god knows how many containers of food. He really hoped she didn't bring the Christmas puddings.

Then Patrick's eyes narrowed on the other new person he hadn't seen before and… wow!

As Patrick stared at the amazing man at Megan's side, his mouth dropped open a little bit and he felt sweat drip off his palms and back.

Patrick couldn't believe how amazing this Mystery Man looked with his tight black shirt, dark brown eyes and stunning cheekbones. He looked amazing, perfect even.

The more he stared, the more Patrick felt his cheeks warm up and he knew he had to talk to this Mystery Guy. He was stunning, and tall!

So Patrick pushed himself off the wall and went over to talk to this amazing, perfectly beautiful Mystery Guy in case this would be another Christmas miracle.

***

Walking along the massive white corridor, passing pictures and other offices, Percy definitely understood now why he was bought along. He was certain all that stuff about Missy and Megan wanting him to find a boyfriend was all just a smoke screen.

Megan just wanted the help for her food.

Percy could hear the Christmas songs playing from here and all that hopefulness and joy was hardly helping him right now as he held container after container of party food for Megan.

Granted she was holding tons too (which surprised Percy) so they were both struggling up the corridor. But the food did smell great, Percy loved the smell of the light sponges, sweet Christmas puddings and all the other food Megan had cooked in his kitchen.

After a few more moments of struggling, Percy

rolled his eyes as he saw two large glass doors to their office but they were closed.

"Guys, food!" Megan shouted.

And if by magic (or everyone knowing how stubborn and bossy Megan was), the door opened and they went inside.

Percy was struggling with all the containers too much to focus on the large office and everyone in the middle dancing as he followed Megan towards the food table. He set the containers on the floor and passed them to Megan in her black dress (that made some straight guys stare at her).

"Isn't this wonderful?" Megan said, sounding more and more excited by the minute.

Percy wished he could share her excitement but he had just struggled to move containers full of amazing food from his car, up tens of flights of stairs (because lifts would spoil the food apparently) and along the corridor. Percy would love to meet anyone who could stay Christmas-y after all that. So Percy knew it would take him a little while to get his Christmas spirit back after all that.

But as he listened to the Christmas songs, saw all the people enjoying the party and breathing in the delicious smell of the food, Percy supposed it wouldn't take long.

"Pers pass me-" Megan said as Percy passed her the (horrible) Christmas puddings.

Percy knelt down to pick up the last of the doomed Christmas puddings and when he stood out up he never expected to see the gorgeous man standing in front of him.

Percy's eyes instantly widened as he stared at the round little face with dark green eyes and short ginger hair. Percy had never known himself to be into red haired men before, but Mr gorgeous definitely convinced him otherwise.

Before he knew it, Percy had quickly looked the gorgeous man up and down. Admiring the man's shiny black shoes, tight trousers and his tight baby blue shirt that was hiding a ripped body underneath.

Mr Gorgeous was just that. Gorgeous.

Percy felt like he wanted to speak but his mind went blank and he only wanted to focus on the beautiful man in front of him. He didn't want to focus on Christmas songs, the other people or even the container of horrible Christmas puddings in his hand.

He only wanted to look at Mr Gorgeous.

"Pers! Pass me the last puds please," Megan said. Making Percy instantly come out of his trance and pass the container over to Megan.

As soon as he had given Megan the container, Percy looked into Mr Gorgeous' amazing dark green eyes and found the courage to talk to him.

"Hi," Percy said before his mouth went dry and again he got lost in Mr Gorgeous' dark eyes.

"Hey I'm Patrick," Mr Gorgeous said holding out his hand.

"Percy," he said as he shook *Patrick's* hand slowly

and he noticed they were both gently rubbing each other's hands like it was the last time they would ever touch. Percy didn't want that, he wanted to touch a lot more, but a simple handshake would have to be enough. He loved the feeling of his skin tingle and the electricity flow between them as they touched for the first, but hopefully not the last time.

"Pers you found Patty. Brilliant!" Megan said as she squeezed past the two men before disappearing into the crowd of dancing people who were now dancing to *Rocking Around The Christmas Tree*.

"Please tell me she didn't bring her puddings," Patrick asked.

Percy smiled. "Sadly. I wanted to bin them. Sorry,"

"No problem. I always let my dogs eat them,"

Percy's eyes narrowed on gorgeous Patrick, he did like dogs and animal lovers, especially red hair animals lovers, were hot. Percy kept taking steps forwards until him and Patrick were slightly away from the food table, so they could talk a little more without possible Megan interruptions.

"What kinds?" Percy asked. In reality he had no idea about dogs, he wouldn't have known a Jack Russel from a bulldog, but this gorgeous man was interesting and Percy didn't want to stop talking to him.

"Two bulldogs and a Yorkshire terrier," Patrick said. "Want to see them?"

As much as Percy wanted him to mean take him

back to his place and show him, Percy sadly knew what he meant so Percy nodded. And instantly wanted to kick him for acting or having such a dirty thought after just meeting the man. He wanted to know why he was acting like this but he was scared he already knew the answer.

When Patrick got out his phone, he showed Percy photos of the cute dogs and Percy loved feeling Patrick's body warmth when he *accidentally* pressed himself against him.

Patrick didn't back away.

Normally Percy would have cursed or panicked whenever he even wondered about doing this to a hot man, but being so close to Patrick felt so natural, even good, even perfect.

"Pers!" Megan shouted from across the dance floor and waving him over.

Percy frowned and looked a couple of times between Megan and Patrick before knowing he should probably go and see what she wanted.

He looked back at gorgeous Patrick, wishing this moment would never end.

"I'm sorry she needs me,"

Patrick gave Percy a sad smile. "It's okay. I'm not going anywhere,"

Percy wanted to think about his words and saviour them but Megan shouted his name again.

But he hoped, prayed, whatever that Patrick wasn't going anywhere.

***

As he watched that utterly stunning man walk off through the dance floor as they were literally *Rocking Around The Christmas Tree*, Patrick felt his heart drop as he realised that that magical moment of chemistry and staring into those amazing eyes was over.

Patrick breathed in the amazing smells of the food mixed in with the scents and hints of the strong aftershaves and perfumes of the other people, and he pressed his back against the warm wall next to the massive food table.

He supposed he should go into the dance floor and join in all the fun but for the first time ever in the history of his Christmas parties, he didn't feel like it. He didn't want to move, he didn't want to eat or dance. He just wanted to stay here where that stunningly beautiful Percy could find him.

Patrick wanted to laugh at himself because out of all his past boyfriends and even a few girls when he was straight, he had never felt like this. He felt like he had just met the most amazing person ever and now they were gone.

Patrick knew it didn't make sense but he had felt the power, electricity and chemistry between him and Percy. He wanted that feeling again and again and again so it would never end.

As Patrick looked across the dance floor, listened to the Christmas songs playing and breathed in the amazing smell of the food, Patrick knew that he was really wasn't going anywhere. He would wait, try some of the horrible Christmas puddings and wait just in case Percy came back to him.

Whether it was for the rest of the night or just longer, Patrick would wait. Just in case it was a Christmas miracle.

***

After gliding his way through the crowd of people enjoying themselves on the dance floor, dancing, drinking and eating. The air was starting to smell of sweat with hints of the perfume and aftershave from the dancing people, but Percy saw Megan in her black dress talking to a tall attractive man in a black suit as she sipped her cocktail.

"What's up Meg?" Percy asked.

"Pers. What's going on with my famous puddings?"

Percy tried not to frown at her. He had been loving his moment with Patrick and she disturbed him for some news about her horrible puddings.

"No one's tried them," Percy said.

"No! Oh my god, people don't know what they're missing. They're perfect,"

Percy gave a sideward glance to the other man and he shrugged. Everyone in the office knew not to touch Megan's puddings.

"Daniel you have to try a pudding," Megan said to the other man.

"Sorry Meggy, I think my wife's calling me," the other man said as he rushed off holding his turned off phone to his ear.

"Pers I'm starting to think people don't like my

puddings,"

Percy hugged her. "Megan,"

As Percy released her from the hug, he breathed in her flowery perfume and looked gently into her large brown eyes.

"What's wrong Pers?"

"You know we all love you but your puddings... they're awful,"

Percy was expecting for some grand argument why they're the best things ever but he was surprised when he saw her nodding and look to the floor.

"Pers. I... I just wanted people to like me and I need to be helpful,"

Percy laughed a little. "Meg, everyone here loves you. Everyone thinks you're amazing and you really interrupted me with Patrick,"

He was expecting to say the last part but now he had said it Percy was going with it.

Megan cocked her head, her eyes narrowing on Percy.

"Really Pers? You were only talking,"

Percy shook his head. "Yes but... he's a great guy. He's hot, beautiful and kind. I..."

As he trailed off, Percy realised he really cared about Patrick, he had come here tonight looking for new friends and maybe a boyfriend (but mainly as muscle for Megan's food containers).

Yet as Percy looked at Megan and saw her infectious smile, he knew he hadn't found a friend, a boyfriend, he had found something a lot more precious.

A soul mate.

A person to spend Christmas with, laugh with and love with. Percy couldn't believe he was thinking this, he hadn't thought about anyone like this before, but he was being honest with himself. Something he rarely did.

And he really wanted Patrick. Hopefully not just for the night, Christmas but hopefully a lot longer.

Megan placed a gentle warm hand on Percy's cheek.

"You're wrong about my puddings. But go and be with Patrick,"

"Really?"

"Yes. I'll get Daniel to drive me home,"

Percy was about to thank her before Megan rushed off into the dancing crowd in the middle of the office.

"Daniel!" Megan shouted.

A tiny part of Percy didn't know what he had just inflicted onto poor Daniel, but none of that mattered. As Percy breathed in the warm air with all the hints of perfume, aftershave and food. He looked across the dance floor and saw the most amazing sight imaginable.

He saw Patrick staring straight at him, smiling and waiting. Percy felt a wave of pure excitement travel up his spine and into his head (and wayward organs) as he felt surprised that this gorgeous stunning man had waited for him.

Percy glided through the crowd and saw Patrick walk towards him, and Percy knew that this was going to be a great Christmas and hopefully a lot, lot longer.

JOURNALIST, ZOOKEEPER, LOVE

If he was a normal person then Journalist Isaac Lee might have waited to write this great new story for his magazine until the summer, or at the very least the spring, because it would have been a lot warmer, nicer and calmer for going to a zoo.

But one of Isaac's many problems was that he was always impatient and he had said to his editor-in-chief that *no one writes about zoos in the winter. Everyone will love it.*

As Isaac drove calmly down the motorway in his little black car, dark clouds gathered overhead, the biting cold outside was seeping into his car and there was definitely not the weather for going to a zoo, but the zoo still wanted him to go and write up a piece about them.

Isaac couldn't believe how cold his hands were, his breath was condensing in front of his eyes and the sweet piney smell of his air refresher was making him feel like he was in some Norwegian forest rather than the English countryside.

As much as Isaac had loved his trips to Norway with his ex-boyfriend. Isaac just wanted to leave that part of him behind himself, he didn't want to focus on the past and all the pain that that had bought his way. He didn't want to think about walking in on his boyfriend in bed with two other men.

He just wanted to focus on his future and his little promotion to Editor of the Nature Section of the magazine he worked at.

All Isaac had wanted was to write about the zoos during the winter months because despite the amazingly bitter cold, these wonderful places still did their best to provide care, love and food for the animals.

And that's what Isaac wanted to highlight. Zookeepers were all amazing people.

Ideally, his story would be the start of something great. If he worked hard, wrote great articles then he might be able to get a job working for a national paper and then maybe grow and climb up the ranks. Maybe becoming an Editor-In-Chief one day.

It would definitely stop the quiet jokes, looks of disappointment and shock his family always had for him whenever he mentioned his job. As far as his family was concerned he was a failure for becoming a little unknown journalist that had no hope of getting a real job.

Isaac really enjoyed the wonderful forests that lined the motorway as he kept driving along. There were thankfully no other drivers on the road which made him feel a lot safer, these poor conditions would always cause an accident and Isaac really didn't want that.

He had a deadline, and there was no chance in hell he was going to miss it.

Yet the real reason why he had hounded his Editor-In-Chief to let him go and arrange a meeting with this particular zoo (and why he didn't tell his family) was because the *Kentish Family Zoo* once belonged to his family.

Apparently according to family tradition that his parents had done their best to stamp out, the zoo once belonged to Isaac's great-Grandmother who was forced to sell the zoo in the 40s after the second world war.

His Great-Grandmother loved it so much, she loved her animals and even though she died long before it was a common practice. But she always made sure to encourage the animal's natural behaviours, as it was now called Animal Enrichment.

Isaac really wished he had met his amazing Great-Grandmother but she died in the 1960s of cancer and barely wrote anything down about her life, the zoo and what it was really like there. All Isaac had were the tales of his grandmother, and her own memory was slowly turning against her.

To Isaac's utter dismay.

Isaac saw a large sign of the Kentish Family Zoo up ahead, and he felt his stomach filled with butterflies. He had to get the story right and he had to make it good enough.

As much as he wanted to believe the magazine he worked for loved the idea of a Nature section, he still couldn't help but feel like it was a stitch-up.

It was no small secret that some rather hot men in tight expensive suits had been visiting the magazine's office every day for the past month. There were rumours of a buy out and merger coming.

And that meant only one thing.

That people were going to be made reductant and all their future stories were going to die with their jobs. Isaac didn't want to become one of those people.

Isaac popped on the indicator and was filled with complete excitement as he turned into the Kentish Family Zoo car park.

He just knew this was going to be an amazing day.

***

Zookeeper Roman Murphy seriously loved his animals. They were honestly the best things in the entire world to him, his animals were behaved, loved and just hilarious.

Roman held a large black bucket filled with chopped up carrots, lettuce and broccoli as he fed by hand some of the tiny goats that the zoo had.

These were probably some of his favourite animals in the entire zoo. They were so cute, small and wonderful animals that were just funny if you watched them for long enough. And unlike other animals they were nice eaters, as well as they didn't want to constantly chop off your fingers!

Yet one of the biggest lies about being a zookeeper had to be how you would get use to the smell after a while. Roman had been working here for three years now and the slight smell of animal spit, poo and urine was something he would never get used to.

Roman liked listening to the constant roaring, birds singing and shrieking of all the animals all over the zoo as they spoke to one another. Roman had been ordered to let them all out for a few hours today as the weather was marginally okay compared to the other days.

Because it was the dead of winter, the animals were kept mostly indoors these days but Roman liked making sure the animals could go outside once every few weeks to help them get some fresh air.

And it seemed to make the beautiful animals of the zoo extremely happy. Roman loved seeing them all and hearing them happy and talking.

Roman finished up feeding the goats their breakfast and looked at his small watch on his wrist. He really didn't want to go and meet the journalist he had been assigned. The journalist was probably some jumped-up awful person who just wanted to destroy the zoo so some housing developer could build on the land.

The zoo was losing money, had had some crimes

and bad leadership recently. But Roman loved this place and he knew that all the criminals had been sorted out now, and he wasn't going to let some jump-up arrogant journalist destroy the place he loved.

Roman took a deep delightful breath of the animal-scented air and went along the concrete pathway down to the reception area which was housed in a large wooden hut.

The walk took him five minutes but he got to get glimpses of the smiling, talking animals having fun despite the biting cold of the entire zoo.

Roman went into the wooden hut, went to the wooden desk that served and the reception area and... fuck!

Roman just stared at the fucking amazing looking guy seating on one of the black chairs. He had such a round handsome face with the cutest little button nose ever, well-styled brown hair and even though he wasn't smiling, he looked so, so gorgeous.

And to make things even worse, Roman couldn't believe that this gorgeous hunk of a man was wearing dirty trousers, an old t-shirt and jumper. He clearly knew that zookeeping wasn't a clean job and he actually looked like he wanted to get involved.

Roman had never ever met a journalist like that.

Granted he was clearly crazy to do his interview or whatever this was in the dead of winter. But if he got cold Roman certainly wouldn't mind warming him up.

Wait!

Roman forced himself to focus on the zoo. Regardless of how hot this man was, he had to focus on his making sure this evil journalist didn't destroy the zoo he loved, he had to protect it.

No matter what.

But damn, this man was hot!

***

Isaac hadn't been waiting too long as he checked his emails, informed his boss that he had arrived safely and everything when he had received a bunch of newspaper clippings from another paper about all the criminal trouble the zoo had been facing.

Isaac was just stunned at what had happened from thief to embezzlement to selling animals on the black market as he sat on the perfectly comfortable black chair.

These stories were amazing and now his boss wanted him to write a story about the zoo now from the perspective of its criminal past. He didn't want to do that.

Isaac had read all the recent reviews of the place when he was waiting to be checked-in, so many people loved this place. They were happy, enjoying themselves and so many of them wanted it to succeed.

Why should Isaac destroy all that?

"Mr Lee?" a man asked.

Isaac put his phone away, stood up and... wow!

Isaac had been expecting some kind of

overweight, ugly zookeeper who was just here to show him round and then kick him out. But this man was… something from another planet with his strong jawline, broad shoulders and drop dead amazing smile.

The man was clearly hot as hell and Isaac was almost scared to talk to him. In fact he couldn't. All his words were trapped in his throat, this story was going to fail completely if Isaac couldn't ask questions.

Isaac had to slowly force himself to talk or just say something or the hot man might just walk off in search for the journalist.

"Hi," Isaac said.

It was all he could force out and he felt like such an idiot.

But the hot man just smiled and bit his lip. Isaac already felt sweat drip down his legs despite how biting cold it was.

The hot man gestured Isaac to follow him and Isaac definitely did that. The hot man led Isaac out of the building and he led him down a very, very long concrete path allowing Isaac to see lions, tigers and bears.

"I'm Roman," the hot man said. "I just want to clarify something first of all,"

Isaac nodded. He was too stunned at the sexiness of his name to speak.

"I will help you with your story and everything, but I will *not* let you destroy this place,"

Isaac stopped for a moment before he quickly caught up with Roman.

"I'm not here to destroy anything. I just got emailed all the reports but I don't want to focus on them. I just want to focus on this place, its animals and its people," Isaac said.

Roman slowly nodded but Isaac just knew he didn't believe him.

After walking and setting out the sort of experiences and information Isaac wanted for his story, Roman led him to the Jaguar enclosure that was filled with large logs, platforms and long grass for the animals to jump and hide in.

Isaac saw a large black jaguar stalk through the grass and another spotted yellow one was peeping out of it. Probably checking out the new visitors he was guessing.

Isaac was a little surprised the jaguars weren't inside, but in a strange way he just sort of sensed that the animals were happy stalking around in the cold for a little while.

"This is Ben and Luke we got them from South America five years ago," Roman said. "Their diet is strictly raw meat but we do give them vitamin supplements and other things to make sure their diet is fully balanced and healthy for them,"

Isaac nodded and made a sure notes of that on his phone just in case he decided to use it in his story.

"And the Jaguar," Isaac said, "was the first ever Olympic Mascot in 1968 in the Mexico games in honour of the Incan culture,"

Isaac smiled as he watched Roman's face drop and smile. Wow, he had such a wonderful smile.

"Um yes," he said. "Not many people know that or find it interesting,"

Isaac's eyebrows rose. "How could they not? The Jaguar and most animals have fascinating histories that I want to highlight in my Nature Section,"

Roman just sort of stood there stunned, and Isaac had to admit he did look so cute in the cold.

"Come with me and I'll get you some real hands-on experiences with the animals," Roman said.

Isaac nodded, but it was amazing to see Roman having to force himself not to extend his hand. Isaac really wanted to hold Roman's hand (and hold a lot more) than that.

But Isaac had to be patient because he wasn't going to screw up this perfect day so far!

***

Roman was completely shocked that Isaac wasn't some jumped-up journalist who wanted to destroy this entire zoo. He was actually rather amazed with this hot sexy hunk of a man, he was interesting, knowledgeable and seemed to really care about the animals.

Even whilst Roman showed him the Orangutans, Lions and Red Pandas, he had been so amazed to see how Isaac was looking at them. Most people just looked at them like they were nice objects to look at and admire for a few moments then move on to the next animal.

But Isaac was different.

He seemed to focus on the animals were the amazing creatures that they were with their own personalities, traits and little quirks that Roman loved too.

After talking, touring and laughing with Isaac for a few hours (and getting Isaac to help him feed the penguins and giraffes), Roman led him to a smaller enclosure that was filled with a large pond, a little wooden hut no bigger than a large doll house and some logs.

This was the Smooth-Coat Otter Enclosure.

Roman had called ahead and gotten one of the other zookeepers to prepare some raw salmon fillets for him, and thankfully the two bowls of them were carefully placed waiting for them.

Roman watched Isaac's face light up as he took some photos, and they both laughed at the three large otters that were tapping away at the fence.

Roman just loved these animals and he was more than glad to see the two stumps near the fence was still upright. They were critical to the feeding process and Roman was so glad he didn't need to somehow get them back upright.

That was a dangerous nightmare at times!

"They know there's food behind it," Isaac said, smiling.

Roman was too impressed with this hunk to say something else. Yet Isaac noticed the two large wooden sticks that they had to use for the otters resting next to a tree.

He picked them up and passed one to Isaac.

After a moment of hesitation he took it and both deeply attractive men went over to the very edge of the Otter enclosure.

"Are these sticks because the otters are so territorial we cannot go in there?" Isaac asked.

Roman didn't know why he was so surprised by him knowing that, but he was. It was so hot and attractive to finally meet another person who knew just as much about animals as him. And seemed to be so happy with it.

Most people (including ex-boyfriends) just thought his work was dull, boring and pointless. But it was so amazing to know that Isaac wasn't one of those people.

"Yes," Roman said, "because we can't go in there. We need to use the sticks to train the animals to stand up and show themselves to us so we can conduct medical checks,"

Isaac nodded and looked fascinated.

"I'll show you," Roman said.

He placed one end of the stick on the ground and tapped it.

A few moments later a very large female otter raced over and touched the end of the stick.

Roman moved the stick to the other side of her and she touched it again.

Then Roman tapped the top of the stump. The

female otter climbed onto the stump, Roman raised the stick higher so the otter had to stretch to touch it.

Roman made the otter hold the position for a few moments then he threw it a piece of salmon.

"So the hold I take it," Isaac asked, "is so you can check it over for medical reasons?"

Roman just nodded and smiled. "Yea. We need to see if there are any lumps, rashes or other things that look concerning. Making the otters hold the position just helps us help them,"

"And it's animal enrichment too," Isaac said.

Wow! Isaac seriously didn't believe this man could get any hotter.

He just had to ask this hot guy out.

The only problem was, did he risk Isaac getting mad, rejecting him and risking the safety of the zoo?

Roman was sure Isaac liked him. But he just couldn't be sure.

***

Isaac completely fell in love with gently tapping the cold ground with the stick in his hand and watching the amazing otters race to it and touch it before they could get their great little treat.

He had read about these types of Otters for years and he had always been slightly interested in them. Because the only main reason why they were endangered was because in south and Southeast Asia the farmers there poured pesticides on their rice crops by the bucketful and then when it rained it washed the pesticides in the rivers, killing the fish and that was what made up most of the Otter's diets.

Isaac loved listening to the otter talk to themselves, beg for more food and just being themselves, and he looked at beautiful sexy Roman and then realised how much he admired him.

He knew that being a zookeeper wasn't all fun and games, but Roman was so lucky to work with these animals day in and out. There were so many remarkable creatures here that Isaac knew somehow that his Great-Grandmother would be damn well proud of her zoo.

It might not have been in his family anymore, but Isaac was delighted to see that the zoo wasn't just surviving. It was thriving.

Isaac almost orgasmed at the feeling of Roman wrapping his arms round his and grabbing his hands to show him how to make the Otters do something else.

Isaac quickly felt something pointy dig into his lower regions, but he hardly minded. He liked it and as Roman said, hold to the otters.

Isaac was surprised that the Otters were gently holding the stick and that allowed Roman and the other zookeepers to check their hands, webbing and fingers.

It was amazing!

With all the salmon fillets used up, Isaac put the stick down and turned around to face the insanely beautiful Roman who was still standing so close to him. Isaac loved how despite the biting cold of the day, he still felt Roman's wonderful warmth radiating towards him.

"And that's the end of the day," Roman said gesturing towards the darkening sky.

Isaac had been having so much fun he hadn't actually realised how dark it was getting, but he did notice one thing. He noticed how sad Roman looked and sounded as he was basically telling Isaac it was time to leave.

"What time does your shift finish!" Isaac blurted out.

Roman gave him a small schoolboy smile. "An hour,"

"I can start my story in the café and wait," Isaac said.

Roman's smile deepened. "Is there something you want to ask me?"

As soon as Roman said it, he looked like he was about to take it back, so Isaac kissed him.

"Will you go out with me?" Isaac asked quickly.

Roman looked around and nodded. "Of course. But I want to know. What will you write in your article?"

Isaac looked back at the happy little family of otters who were snuggling up together after a large feeding. They looked perfectly happy, warm together and like they were in heaven.

After spending so much of the day focusing on the story, zoo and beautiful Roman. Isaac finally knew exactly what he would write.

"I will tell people the truth. This is a wonderful place with happy animals, zookeepers and very hot ones too,"

Roman laughed and Isaac did too.

As Roman guided Isaac back to the wooden hut where the café was also located, Isaac couldn't believe how lucky he was.

He had come here looking for a story, and he was going to leave with a story and something far, far better.

GAY SWEET ROMANCE COLLECTION

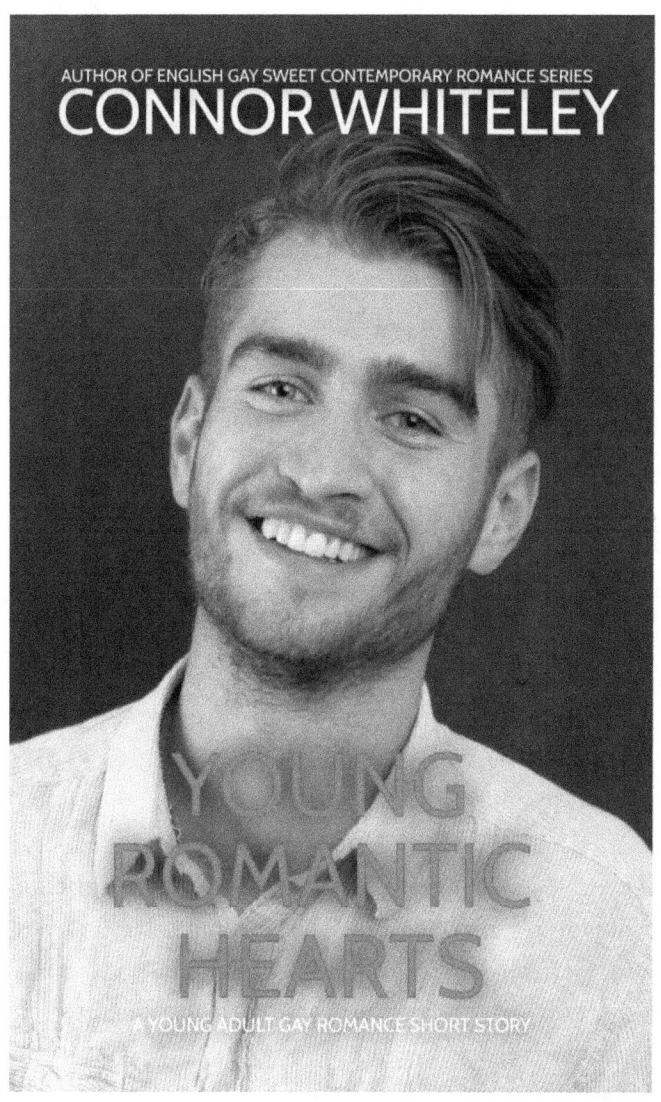

YOUNG ROMANTIC HEARTS

17 year old James had always known he was gay ever since he had started secondary school at 13. Then it didn't take too long to realise that he had really been gay, and he had only pretended or tricked himself into being straight for the sake of his family, friends and school.

But he had just had enough of all that utter rubbish so James had definitely decided to come out last month.

His family reacted like it wasn't news at all and they said they would always love him, his friends again didn't react and they all claimed they already knew. Then as the gossip dripped into the mainstream conversations of the school, everything seemed fine, happy and wonderful. But James had already heard a few homophobic comments in his direction.

James supposed that was life to some extent and with everyone else being so positive and uncaring towards the fact he was gay. He was fine and could definitely deal with a few comments from silly bullies.

It just made James laugh when the younger students came up to him and shouting something homophobic in his face trying to look *hard* for all their mates.

James didn't know whether to laugh, feel sorry or just smile at that. Surely there were better ways to look good in front of your mates than picking on the gay kid?

As James lent against the bright blue lockers of his school in a long corridor with white walls, the horrible blue carpet that schools just had to have apparently and a pair of large reinforced windows that looked down above the canteen area below. James was just waiting for his best friend Livi to come out from class, come to her locker and they could walk home together.

Mr Richards, James's biology teacher, always let them go early at the end of the day. He claimed it was because he liked them all, but everyone knew it was because him and Miss Tyler were seeing each other. And he wanted to get out of class sooner to meet her.

It was nice if not a little strange considering the two acted like they hated each other outside of the classroom.

The smell of sweat, deodorant and perfume filled the corridor and whilst James would never admit it, he wouldn't mind seeing some of the boys that the deodorant belonged to. It smelt amazing.

The winter chill in the air was definitely filtering into the school and James really wanted Livi to hurry up so they could both go home and James could get in the warmth. But he was a bit concerned that Livi was plotting something for him and their group of friends.

James had been way too focused on an eighteen year old in the same year as him at lunchtime, but he had managed to hear that Livi was talking about going out tonight.

As much as James loved her and the rest of his friends, he really wasn't sure about going out-out tonight with his mates. Especially in this winter chill, but if her offer was good enough he might as well as go.

"Fairy!" a little 14 year old girl shouted as she ran down the corridor.

James just smiled and shook his head. If these people were going to try and make him feel bad why couldn't they create some more original slurs?

And surely these younger (and older) students knew that not all gays were feminine, and James never wanted to be like that. He liked being straight-acting and not looking like a stereotypical gay.

But if people wanted to look like that then James would only support that.

Yet the only major problem about being gay in secondary school was it was even harder to find another gay boy and hope to have a relationship with. All James wanted was to have fun, see a cute boy and kiss him a little.

James had tried to sense his way through secondary school to find another gay boy through the years, but nope. He couldn't find a single one. That either meant that James was truly the only gay in the school, or the others were a lot better at hiding in than he ever thought possible.

The sound of tons of students talking, running and shouting made James move to the other side of the corridor as Livi with her slim body, long wavy hair and long black skirt came over to James holding her large pink school bag.

James and her started to walk down the corridor when Livi gave him a dirty smile.

"What?" James asked.

"Wanna go out tonight with the gang?" Livi asked.

"What's the offer?"

Livi smiled and shook her head. James knew she was thinking him as difficult but it was part of their fun, banter and all the other stuff that young peeps got up to.

"You, me and the gang going to the Christmas Fair at dockside later on. I'm driving and there's a new boy joining us. You're going with him,"

James couldn't help but grin. That's what this was really about, clearly Livi was far better at scouting out other gays than he was. That was just embarrassing.

"Should note," Livi said. "He isn't gay. He's my

ex and we needed another driver to get us all there, so he's picking you up at five,"

James loved how Livi had basically no organisation skills and just assumed that he was free and perfectly able to get there without his family planning anything tonight.

"You coming?" Livi asked as they walked down the stairs.

James rolled his eyes. He did need to go out and it would be fun going to the fair with his friends, and he might see a cute boy there too.

So what did he have to lose?

"Yes," James said.

Livi hugged him and they almost fell down the stairs.

***

17-year-old Harry really wasn't sure about going tonight as he drove his little black car down a wonderfully wide narrow street with large houses on either side and plenty of parked cars in the road. He had only passed his test a few months ago so he was still getting used to it. But he did love the freedom of driving.

Harry smelt the slight hints of vanilla coming from his car air fresher that his mum had bought him for passing his test. She was always doing weird little gifts for him in different ways, but it was one of the things he loved about her.

Harry wasn't sure about going tonight with Livi and her friends. Their relationship hadn't exactly ended perfectly because he had broken it off. Harry had said he was breaking it off because she deserved better (which was true) but in reality it was because he wasn't sure he was into girls in the slightest.

When he had been going out with Livi, it had been amazing, wonderful and they had had a lot of fun together. But after a month Harry was noticing how much effort he was putting into faking it all.

He didn't want Livi to be with a faker. So he ended it.

Harry turned a corner and started driving down a very curvy road.

With Livi picking up the rest of her friends, Harry had been sent to pick up a boy called James. He had seen him around school a few times, but never really focused on him. He knew he was the gay boy at school and he had to admit, he did hate it when other people picked on him.

There was just no reason for it, but Harry was already starting to regret his choice of clothing for the evening.

When Livi had called Harry, he had told her he was busy with football practice tonight, but she had insisted that he come, so he agreed. But as he drove in his black Adidas tracksuit, football boots and activewear t-shirt. He was seriously starting to doubt if he was going to be warm enough.

If any luck he might find a cute boy to warm up with him.

Well, Harry wasn't sure what he wanted. All he

knew was that he wasn't into girls anymore and wasn't entirely sure he was into boys yet either.

After a few more minutes of driving, Harry pulled outside James's house which was a wonderfully large good-looking one with large crystal clean windows, a very well maintained rose garden out front and a gravel pathway to a black front door.

Harry didn't know what he should do really, because he was a few minutes early. He didn't know James so it would be a little weird if he just went up to his door, wouldn't it?

Should he get Livi to text him he was outside?

After a few more seconds of struggling to know what to do, Harry huffed and got out of his car and went straight up to James's door.

He knocked three times.

When the door opened Harry had been expecting James' mum or dad to open it, but when it opened… oh yeah. Harry knew he was into boys without a shadow of a doubt.

James was standing in front of him and he looked so amazing and hot and beautiful in his tight black jeans, tight fitting hoody and his longish blond hair really framed his handsome face perfectly.

Even James' amazing brown eyes were so seductive and alluring that Harry seriously wanted to stare at them all night.

Harry felt his stomach fill with butterflies, his hands went sweaty and a lump was caught in his throat.

Harry was so embarrassed. He had never had a reaction like this to girls, so he was so surprised, shocked and embarrassed that he was having it with a boy.

But James was so beautiful.

This was going to be a great night.

***

Wow!

James had always known Livi dated some pretty hot guys that were bound to be into sports, and he had never ever expected one of Livi's ex to look like this.

James couldn't help himself but stare at the utterly gorgeous man in front of him. James just loved his brown buzzcut haircut that normally didn't work on boys but it seriously worked on this one.

And James couldn't get over how amazing this boy looked in his Adidas tracksuit, footballs and… he was just flat out amazing. James didn't have the words to describe it.

James wanted to hug and kiss the boy so badly, and judging by the schoolboy grin on the boy's face the feeling might be mutual.

But as much as James would seriously love this amazingly hot boy in front of him to be gay, he couldn't do anything, couldn't he? After all this was one of Livi's exes.

"Hi," James forced out after a moment.

James was surprised at how weak he felt inside and standing next to this hot boy.

"Hey," the boy said. "I'm Harry, Livi's ex,"

James could only nod. Livi was so lucky to have him as a boyfriend. Seriously lucky.

"Should we get going?" Harry asked.

James forced himself to concentrate and he had to start acting normal, but James had never felt this attracted to a guy before. He was so, so beautiful.

"Yea," James said, him and Harry went over to his car.

James popped in the passenger's side and it was a great little car. He knew most of the boys at school would have judged Harry as poor or silly to have such a cheap looking car and calling himself a man or boy, but James liked it.

Both him and Harry quickly put on their seat belts.

As Harry turned on the engine and they started driving off, James seriously had to fight the urge not to stare at Harry the entire way. It was a twenty minute drive to the fair, and James was definitely going to make that time pay.

He wasn't going to waste this alone time with such a gorgeous boy for a moment. But he should probably at least get to know him a little first.

"Thanks for picking me up. You have football practice for something?" James asked.

Harry had such a beautiful smile.

"Yeah. I do football practice on the school team just finished practice when I had to come here. I'll probably change when we get there,"

"Please don't," James muttered involuntarily.

"Why not?"

Crap!

James had no idea that he had been that loud or Harry had extremely good hearing. He was so hot and James had just about said the gayest thing he could to this hottie.

"Um," James said trying to think of an answer. "Because I know Livi really wants to see you, and you don't want to delay her do you?"

James saw Harry frown a little and he couldn't help but wonder if Harry had wanted the truer answer, the one about James finding him extremely hot in that sportswear.

"No. No one keeps Livi waiting, do they?" Harry said.

They both laughed and James felt a rush of butterflies fly through him at the amazing sound of James's laugh.

Even if Livi took Harry away from him for the rest of the night, James was definitely going to enjoy and savour these next fifteen minutes with this insanely hot and beautiful boy.

***

After three hours, the amazing fair with all its attractions, lights and music was finally starting to die down and Harry loved it how James hadn't left his side since they got out of the car.

Well, Harry wasn't exactly sure who had been following who. Sometimes it was definitely James, but other times Harry had purposefully got with James on rides that the others didn't want to.

The dodgers were probably Harry's favourite with him and James driving the car together. When another car crashed into James or Harry would crash into the other, and Harry loved it.

They were both constantly laughing, smiling and joking with each other.

One of the great things about dockside was that there was a large wooden pier on the far side of the fair filled with unmanned Grabber Arcade Games.

Right where Harry was standing was in front of a large row of ten of them with a wider range of different themes from Mario to the latest blockbuster to the various superheroes of the different universes. James was trying to get a little superhero themed teddy bear out of the grabber and he was so cute to watch.

The winter chill blew off the river below them and he noticed James was shivering a little in just his hoody. Thankfully Livi and the others had gone home ages ago leaving just him and James alone.

The fair officially closed at nine so they had about another half an hour left, and the wonderful smell of candy floss, mince pies and mulled wine was definitely a reason to stay, even if him and James couldn't have any of the wine.

James huffed as the teddy bear he wanted for some reason slipped out of the Grabber and then the machine stopped working and James just rolled his eyes like he didn't want to play anymore anyway.

As he stood up from playing the machine, Harry felt his heart skip a few beats as James just looked so, so beautiful as the bright arcade lights lit up his handsome beautiful face.

Then Harry and James slowly walked over to the edge of the pier and leant against the icy chilled wooden railing of the pier and stared out over the rough river before them.

There was just something so peaceful, relaxing and perfect about being there with James, Harry never wanted this moment to end. There was just something so romantic about standing here alone together away from all the eyes of the other kids at school and watching the little lights of boats in the river and the lights of houses on the other side.

Harry moved closer to James and rested his head against his shoulder. Harry loved the electricity that zapped between them and James rested his head against his too.

"I don't want tonight to end," Harry said, lifting his head back up and looking into James' stunningly beautiful eyes.

James's smile was equally stunning as his eyes.

"I didn't think Livi picked gay guys," James said, smiling.

Harry laughed. "I didn't either. But I'm enjoyed tonight and... I really don't want it to end,"

James gave Harry a perfect little grin that melted Harry's heart.

"I want to kiss you so badly," James said.

Harry felt his stomach fill with the most butterflies he had ever felt before, he wondered if his stomach was about to burst. He had never done that before.

But Harry looked around, not because he was embarrassed or ashamed of wanting to kiss James, but because deep down he knew he wanted people to see him being his true self.

No one was about.

That was probably for the best considering he hardly needed the gossip going round school if he wanted to become football captain.

But he so badly wanted James to kiss him.

"Go on then," Harry said grinning.

James's smile deepened. "You don't have to say it. I know it could hurt your footballing and-"

Harry wrapped his arms around James and kissed him. Harry had kissed a lot of girls in the past but nothing felt as right as this and wow… James seriously knew how to kiss.

Harry quickly forgot about not wanting this night to end, he really didn't want this amazing kiss to end.

And Harry just knew this was going to be the first passionate kisses of many.

***

A few weeks later after Christmas but before New year, James had his arms wrapped round Harry who was sadly in his amazingly hot jeans and white t-shirt and not his insanely hot sportswear, as they both laid on James' big single bed after having dinner with James's parents, talking about their Christmases and watching a film together.

As the film ended and both the lovers just laid there in silence, James couldn't believe how amazing the past few weeks had been. James had wanted to find another gay boy at school and he really had, he had found a beautiful, hot boy that made him feel amazing and loved.

Something no girl ever could.

And James was amazed and excited and happy to see how Harry had become more confident in the past few weeks. They had spent so much time together and they knew they were never going to get bored of each other, because they really did love each other.

As James had suspected (and it was Harry's idea actually) Livi had always suspected that Harry was actually gay so having him pick up James that night was a part of a plan to make the two boys fall in love. James was amazed that it had worked but he was so, so glad that it had.

Thankfully it turned out that both James and Harry were as romantic as each other, and James loved having someone else making him feel special, beautiful and great whenever they went out.

Even James's parents loved Harry and his parents loved James. That was something that he hadn't expected, he didn't know why. He just did.

So as the film ended it just stopped on the TV

and neither James nor Harry moved. James was more than happy about that because he seriously loved having Harry in his arms and Harry holding him back.

After so many years of hiding himself, lying to himself and just denying himself what he knew was right, James was so happy that he was finally living his truth with such a beautiful sexy man.

James knew that the future was going to be very, very bright and with Harry by his side, James couldn't wait to find out how spectacular it was going to be.

GAY SWEET ROMANCE COLLECTION

HOLIDAY, BURNOUT, LOVE

Benji Michaels had never been one for "falling in love". Lots of people often thought of him as too serious, focused on university and studying to have fun at parties, clubs and more of the partying side of university.

In truth, Benji never believed he was too serious. He only didn't like the drinking side of university. He loved people, hot guys and actually talking to everyone, but he hated with a passion the loud awful music that was pumped so loud he couldn't hear a person standing right next to him.

As Benji sat on the awfully uncomfortable fabric computer chairs at the university library at the very end of the massive row of computers on the top floor, Benji couldn't wait for the Christmas holidays to start in a few hours.

A lot of students had already left, but Benji still had one more biomedical science lecture to attend in the late afternoon before he could officially leave. All his friends had left yesterday, and as much as he wanted to join them. He was a tat too dedicated to his studies.

And as stupid as it sounded, Benji didn't want the poor lecturer to be all alone. If the lecturer was going to put the effort in, then Benji wanted to be kind enough to at least turn up.

The quiet mutters in the distance was the only sound despite the humming, vibrating and slightly popping of the old computers that filled the library. Lots of students would have been drained by the silence, but Benji wasn't.

Unlike other students Benji liked coming to the library for the quiet, it allowed him to concentrate, focus and actually achieve something.

Benji truly loved his parents and younger and older siblings at home, but they were a nightmare when he wanted to achieve something at home.

That's why Benji always came here on Friday afternoons.

The scents of strong flowery perfume with hints of cedarwood, pecans and cloves started to fill the air and leave the taste of Christmas cookies on Benji's tongue, strangely enough, and he instantly knew who was going to turn up sooner or later.

His best friend Victoria Harris always wore way too much perfume, but Benji didn't mind. Her attitudes and friendship more than made up for any problems the overwhelming smell caused.

The computer beeped as Benji opened up his

university emails and saw one from a slightly older university student. A senior, a year ahead of Benji, who Benji had to admit was very fit, hot and sexy.

Benji had always had a thing for Ezra Hawks ever since he had met him a few months ago when a professor Benji was helping out his year introduced them. Benji had no idea whatsoever if Ezra was into men, but he was hot.

All Benji could do was bit his lip at the idea of them two talking, laughing and spending time together.

As Victoria had said, they barely knew each other, but Benji had spoken to Ezra a few times and he always made Benji feel like a schoolboy, happy and alive.

Victoria tried to understand, but Benji knew she didn't. And he couldn't blame her, how do fall for a guy you barely know?

As Benji tried to forget about those doubts, he read the email and hoped it was a response to the work Benji had submitted to Ezra to get his opinion on. Since Benji was hardly the best student on essays (it was the so-called writing style that he struggled with the most) and he really hoped Ezra would want to meet up and give him some tips.

To Benji's frustration, Ezra had agreed to give some feedback but not in-person. Benji just smiled at his little attempt to see the hot sexy man in person, but it had failed.

But at the end of the day, Benji was just happy

for any guidance Ezra could give him.

Yet to Benji's surprise the email was rather coldly written compared to normal, and it was a very formal apology saying that Ezra didn't have time to give feedback this side of the Christmas holidays, and he would do it next year.

Benji finished the email and just felt like there was something more to it. He was partly glad that Victoria wasn't here yet because she probably would have said he was overthinking it.

But Benji had spoken, email and met Ezra plenty of times, and in every single email Ezra was a delight to talk to. Something else was going on, and even though Benji wasn't even friends with him, he still wanted to find out more.

As Victoria's heavy high heels pounded towards Benji, he just looked at the tall, beautiful brunette that was his best friend.

Thankfully she was good friends with Ezra and Benji really wanted her to do some spying for him.

***

Ezra Hawks had always wanted to go to university ever since he was a young teenager. He wanted to develop his knowledge, get a degree and get a professional job so he could help as many people as he possibly could.

That was one of the advantages of doing biomedical science. There were so many jobs you could do that paid very well and helped a lot of great people too.

But as Ezra stood in one of the university's many cafes with its rows upon rows of little tables, booths and a few other students sitting around. Ezra just wished he wasn't so committed to his studies, he wished he wasn't here anymore and he was home.

So many of his friends had already gone home and as much as Ezra wanted to do that. He felt like he wanted to do a lot more than just leave university for the Christmas Holidays. He was seriously considering giving up for good.

Ezra rather liked the scents of coffee, hot chocolate and cinnamon that filled the air as all other students bought their fuel to keep them going until the end of the university day.

Ezra stood holding his own hot chocolate and he was just enjoying the warmth radiating from it, and considering his future.

He had been working so hard so late. Reading as much as he could, working as much as possible on his dissertation and everything else that was expected of a first-class final year student.

And he hated it. Ezra had been throwing up from the stress for the past three nights. He hadn't been eating and he had lost half-a-stone recently too.

Ezra didn't feel rubbish, but he felt like that was a dangerous sign too.

Yet the most concerning thing of all of his troubles, was Ezra didn't have anyone to talk to. Ezra couldn't talk to his amazing friends because they were all doing great and loving life. He couldn't talk to his family because he didn't want to admit failure, and most of his family believed in it was first-class grades or nothing. And Ezra didn't want to tell his professors in case he looked bad.

Ezra was burned out, trapped and didn't know where to go.

A group of friends laughing as they walked out of the café made Ezra smile briefly. He wanted to do that with his friends but he knew sooner or later they would talk about their projects and he would feel terrible.

Ezra had felt bad enough emailing that sweet boy Benji earlier and telling him he couldn't look at his work this year.

Benji was such a sweet wonderful guy that Ezra did want to get to know better. There was something so innocent, cute and adorable about him. Ezra loved Benji's little button nose, boyish grin and stunning emerald green eyes.

And strangely enough, Ezra just felt so at home around him. Sure, he had only met Benji a few times, but he loved each of those times.

It was just a shame Ezra didn't feel like he could tell anyone, because he didn't want to be judged. And surely a relationship could never work out with Ezra perhaps moving to another university after his undergraduate degree?

"Hey Ez," Victoria said as she hugged Ezra.

Ezra was a little surprised to still see her here. He took Victoria for the type of girl that would leg it from university the second she could. But it was great seeing her.

Probably one of his only true friends.

"Thought you would have left yet," Ezra said.

Victoria weakly smiled. "Well I thought so to. I have a lecture later but wanted to skip it, but Benji convinced me to stay,"

Ezra forced himself not to shiver in delight as she said Benji's name. To his annoyance, because he never acted like this with anyone else, Ezra felt the urge to go to Benji, talk to him just so Ezra could feel at home and relax.

It was so strange how he could just do that so naturally around Benji. He didn't know why but he did.

"Is he okay about me not looking at his bits?" Ezra asked.

Ezra almost blushed about looking at Benji's *bits*. But he managed to stay professional, yet he'd been lying if he said the idea hadn't crossed his mind.

Victoria's smile deepened. "You know you can do no wrong in his eyes. He's sweet on you and you know it. And what's wrong?"

Ezra didn't want to hear about Benji's feelings. He wasn't sure he felt the same and he really didn't want to do anything that would end up hurting Benji later on.

"What you mean *up with me*?" Ezra asked.

Victoria forced herself to sigh.

"Darling Ez. Come on, you don't send Benji

formally cold emails. What's wrong?"

Ezra bit his lip. He didn't think he had been that obvious, but he really wanted to sound like he liked and was interested in Benji, just in case he felt the same.

Ezra wanted to kick himself for acting like this, maybe he was a lot more interested in Benji than he thought. But he couldn't get involved with him. Not with Ezra struggling with university.

That wasn't fair on either of them.

But maybe Victoria could help.

Ezra carefully took Victoria over to one side of the little café and told her about him struggling, being sick and not wanting to get Benji involved or hurt by a guy like him.

Victoria hugged him. "Benji might be good for you then. He likes you a lot. He might be some good stress relief if you get what I mean,"

Ezra really liked the idea of that, but he couldn't bring himself to do it.

And then Ezra just looked around the university café and realised he really didn't like any of this. He didn't like the university, the work and the rest of it, and he just wanted to escape it all for a little while.

Christmas was a week tomorrow so if he really wanted it, he could escape for a week and relax. He could go travelling, see the sites of England he had always wanted to see and there were always cheap deals around so it was possible.

Ezra really smiled at the idea of travelling. He

loved seeing different places, experience new things and it would give him the space to know what he wanted out of life.

"What?" Victoria asked.

Ezra slowly looked at her. "I'm going to travel for a week. I'll leave tonight and I'll know by Christmas what I want from my life,"

Ezra was hoping Victoria would look happy for him, but she didn't. Her face sort of dropped and Ezra instantly felt bad.

Victoria probably looked like that because Ezra had never been much of the spontaneous type. Normally he was an extreme planner, and the idea of him going travelling was probably unthinkable.

But it was what Ezra needed and as much as he loved her as a friend she wasn't going to stop him from doing this and making a decision.

And he told her so and kissed her on the head.

***

Benji stood up next to his computer on the top floor of the university library and stared out of the massive floor-to-ceiling windows out over the freezing cold campus. He really didn't want Victoria to tell him anything bad was happening, but he was really concerned about Ezra.

Without a shadow of a doubt Benji knew how silly he was for being concerned, because he barely knew Ezra at the end of the day. But he couldn't help but feel like there was a connection between them.

A connection Benji wanted to explore so, so

badly.

"We have a problem," Victoria said and she quickly told Benji about Ezra struggling of late.

Benji completely failed to hide his surprise. Ezra had always been so confident, hot and sexy whenever anyone spoke to him that Benji never would have imagined he was struggling with university.

"And I think he's going to quit university," Victoria said.

Benji's eyes just widened. "But Ezra has always wanted to help others. He wanted to become a first responder or paramedic. If he quits he would throw his life away,"

Benji was surprised at the small beads of sweat dripping down his face. He didn't want Ezra to do this, he wanted him to stay at the university and complete his degree.

He just knew that if Ezra left now then he would never forgive himself and Ezra would be doomed doing jobs he never wanted to do.

His life would be miserable.

But most importantly, Benji wanted Ezra to stay so he could see his beautiful face, amazing body and that killer smile that always made him feel so much better.

"How do I stop him?" Benji asked.

Victoria shrugged. "Don't know if you can,"

"I have to," Benji said, "I have to try. Ezra needs to stay. I…"

Victoria took a few steps closer. "I what?"

Benji focused on the small snowflakes that were starting to fall across the university campus.

"I... I care about him and I would never forgive myself if I didn't try," Benji said.

Victoria smiled. "Don't you think you're being a bit selfish?"

Benji threw his arms up in the air. She was being impossible.

"No!" Benji shouted. "This isn't about me. This is about all the people Ezra will never help,"

Victoria started laughing.

"What?" Benji asked.

Victoria hugged him. "That's how you convince him to stay, and I told him you're sweet on him,"

Benji rolled his eyes. He didn't want her to tell him that, and seriously, saying he was *sweet* on him made Benji sound so old. But maybe there was a point to this.

"How did he react?" Benji asked.

Victoria shrugged and started to walk away.

"He didn't my dear. And I have a train to catch and you have a man to save. Happy Christmas and see you in the new year Ben,"

As annoying as Victoria could be, he did love her as a friend. She could be mystic, uncaring and completely not dedicated to her studies, but she was probably the best of friends he could ask for.

And she was right.

Benji quickly packed up his things and raced off to find Ezra.

He had to stop him.

***

Ezra was really looking forward to travelling up to the lake district for a week to help clear his head. He was really looking forward to walking through the amazing hills, looking at the wonderful lakes and just being far from urban areas and in nature without another person around.

Ezra still smiled at what his parents had said earlier when he phoned them. They were proud of him for knowing what was right for him, they would love him no matter what or they were concerned about him.

He was concerned about himself too.

As Ezra popped open the booth of his little black car that was still parked at the university, he started to put his laptop inside and his stomach started to get tighter and tighter.

Ever since Victoria had told him that Benji liked him he couldn't stop thinking about it. Ezra loved how sweet, caring and great-looking Benji was.

He was almost tempted to ask Benji to join him for the week, but wasn't that wrong? Wasn't this week away meant to be about being alone and thinking about what was right for his future?

No. Ezra couldn't invite Benji.

His stomach tightened again as he closed the booth and the cold dampness of the weather increased as small snowflakes started snowing down. Ezra didn't know how cold it was going to get in the

Lake District, but at least he would be alone and able to think.

Before Ezra got in his car, he took a final look round the university and he wasn't sure if he would be back. He loved it here, he loved the learning and the people, but it just wasn't agreeing with him.

Ezra had already been sick again as he was coming out to his car (thankfully the bathrooms were close by).

The fresh vanilla scent from his car air refresher made Ezra smile as he got into his car, closed the door and started the engine.

He was leaving the university and he properly wasn't going back.

Ezra had to admit it would have been great to get to know Benji better, see him smile and even asked him out on a date. But Ezra couldn't bring himself to start a relationship with that sweet man if Ezra wasn't going to continue at university.

It just didn't seem fair.

Ezra looked about and started reversing out of the parking bay.

He hit something.

"Ouch!"

There was something so familiar and sexy about the person who shouted out, but Ezra quickly got out of his car and his hands covered his mouth when he saw he had hit Benji.

The cute sexy man was just laying there on the biting cold ground holding his ankle and hissing out in pain. Ezra lifted him up and Ezra loved the feeling of Benji's hard smaller body against his, and Ezra helped Benji into the passenger front side.

Ezra quickly ran round to the other side and he sat in the driver's seat.

"I'm so sorry," Ezra said.

After a few moments, Benji started laughing as the pain was clearly starting to ease off.

"It's probably my fault too. I sort of race out to get you before you left,"

Ezra rubbed his eyebrows. He couldn't believe that Victoria ran straight to Benji, the very man he was trying to spare the feelings of. He didn't want to do this but he was clearly going to have to be straight with such a beautiful man.

"Benji I-" Ezra said.

"Wait. Listen," Benji said. "I know you're struggling but you'll pass. That's all that matters. You don't need to be a first class student for everyone, all you have ever wanted to do was help people and become a paramedic or first responder,"

Ezra nodded. He didn't know why he had forgotten that, he had been so focused on pleasing his parents and family that he had forgotten why he was doing this in the first place.

Benji hissed as he moved his ankle and he leant closer to gently rub Ezra's hands. Ezra couldn't believe how amazing it felt to have Benji holding and rubbing his hands.

"And all I want for you is to be happy and do

what you want with your life. Even if you don't want me," Benji said.

Ezra didn't know what to say.

Of course he wanted to go out with Benji, see what their relationship would bring and everything and it was amazing that he actually cared about Ezra as much as he did.

Ezra just…

Benji kissed him. Ezra loved the amazing softness and sweetness of his lips against his.

Then Benji pulled away and gestured that he was getting out of the car.

"Sorry. Just wanted that in case you do leave," Benji said.

Benji popped open the door but Ezra grabbed his hand. Ezra couldn't leave the university, his future or this beautiful man without at least trying out a relationship.

And Ezra couldn't think of a better way to test out a relationship than going away together. He had already paid for the room and it did come with a large double bed.

"Come with me. Please," Ezra said.

He was expecting Benji to say no, leave him and protest something rotten.

But he just smiled, got back in the car and kissed Ezra again.

It was the first of many passionate kisses before they left the university car park.

***

On their last day of their little holiday together Benji stood outside their little wooden hut in the middle of nowhere in the freezing cold. The air was wonderfully crisp with hints of damp, coldness and pine that was so delightful to breathe in.

Benji had left Ezra sleeping in their sensational double bed that had plenty of use over the past week, and Benji actually couldn't believe how perfect the last week had been.

Benji had absolutely loved talking and hiking and exploring with Ezra about everything that they wanted to achieve, their families and the rest. They had both laughed plenty of times about how similar they were, they both grew up in similar places and they just had so much in common.

In one week they had felt such a strong connection to each other, and that connection had only grown in the past week. Benji was really looking forward to the future that they would make together, and that was definitely true.

And thankfully both Benji's and Ezra's families had video called their sons over the holiday so they got to briefly met each other. Benji loved Ezra's family because of their liveliness, energy and personalities. And they loved him according to Ezra.

It was the same for his family.

As Benji felt two wonderfully strong arms wrap around him from behind, he kissed Ezra's arms and turned around. Benji loved Ezra in his posh grey jumper and wonderfully styled hair that Benji had messed up plenty this week.

And they both smiled at each other like lovers and schoolboys do.

Because this was going to be the start of an amazing final day of their holiday, and the start of something much, much longer.

But just as special. If not more so.

HOMELESS, CHARITY, LOVE

Marcus Harris absolutely hated with a passion the classic myth about homeless people. So many uninformed people said that all homeless peeps were just dumb, stupid people who had nothing better to be with their lives.

Marcus hated that myth with a passion, because he had gone to university, had a wonderful flat but that had quickly changed when he was 24 years old and found love.

Ever since he was a young kid, Marcus had just known he was different. This difference was only made more and more extreme in secondary school when all his friends had been talking about the hottest girls and celebrities, and Marcus couldn't see the point of any of it. He was much more interested in talking about the very hot footballers on the school's team.

No one else cared.

Marcus had always felt like something was extremely wrong with them (and according to his family he was flat out insane) but when he went to university at the year of 18 he had slowly realised that he found men very hot.

It didn't take him too long to find out he was gay. Very gay.

In his final year he had met a wonderful man called Robin, they made each other laugh, made love and Marcus honestly wanted to spend the rest of his life with Robin.

That wasn't going to happen.

As Marcus sat on the freezing cold damp concrete under a railway bridge with the smell of urine, poo and rubbish filling the air. Marcus truly hated his family for what they did to him, because Marcus had didn't have Robin and he honestly thought his family was perfectly okay with gays.

They seriously weren't.

Robin had been punched, accused of corrupting their son and Robin ran away.

Marcus still felt just as dead inside now as he did a few months ago when it all happened. His soul was almost as cold and numb as his bum on the concrete.

The sound of rain lashing down just made Marcus frown even more. He was cold, thirsty and hungry, like he was most days recently.

Marcus hated how his family had dragged him with a suitcase of some clothes, his laptop and phone to their family car and drove him towards a local Conversion therapy centre.

Marcus didn't want to be conditioned, tortured

or drugged, but because it wasn't illegal in the UK, his family had every legal right to help their son "correct himself". As soon as the car stopped at a set of traffic lights, Marcus charged out of the car and ran as fast as he could.

There was no chance in hell he was going to a conversion therapy centre.

So for the past few months, Marcus had been completely homeless with no clothes, phone or food.

Thankfully, Marcus had learnt quickly about sitting in Canterbury High Street and begging (something that the police hated) for food. But so few people believed he was actually homeless.

Then Marcus hated it even more when the one or two homeless pretenders were there, getting all the real food and money. Marcus had shouted at one of them more than once.

As Marcus listened to the rain continue to lash down, he watched a little stream of rain ran into him, wet his pieces of cardboard he slept on and Marcus just hated his life.

Marcus had tried to get a sleeping bag before but he needed money for that, something he didn't have. He had tried to get a job but he didn't have a bank account. Something he no longer had access to. Marcus had even tried working cash in hand, but that was illegal.

With the rain pounding the railway bridge above him, Marcus truly believed his life was so pointless, silly and he was just a burden on the entire world. He had considered suicide once or twice (with it being December it wouldn't be difficult to die in the cold), but Marcus still had a silly little piece of hope keeping him going.

He just wanted to see Robin one more time.

Marcus couldn't forget how that amazing hot sexy guy made him laugh, smile and feel like his true self, and not some pretender who had had to pretend to be something he had known his entire life.

His stomach roared in frustration and Marcus just had to laugh. If someone looked at his clothes that hung on his bare boned body and scarily thin frame, they never would have imagined he was once a footballer at his university with great muscles, legs and a so-called "killer ass" according to some guys.

He hadn't been that man for ages.

A crippling blast of pain corkscrewed from his stomach to his chest, and Marcus seriously knew he had to get some food.

There had been a rumour of a homeless charity that had popped up recently on the high street, Marcus had to try to make it.

He just didn't know if he was strong enough to make it.

***

Robin Ossam had always loved being gay. He loved men, their minds and their bodies as much as he could when he was younger, and he had definitely carved his way through the university's gay community before he graduated.

As Robin stood behind a large buffet counter filled with hot metal trays of soup, bread and full-fat cream, he was filled with such delight that he could finally do what he loved (besides from men).

Ever since he was young and came out at aged 16, he had heard horrific stories about gay kids being thrown out of their houses, abandoned by their families and forced to live on the cold streets.

So the moment he knew that he was perfectly safe in his own, Robin had volunteered and tried to do as much as he could to help others. He didn't care at all if the homeless person was gay, straight, whatever. He only cared about helping them.

Robin smiled at some of the old military veterans who were helping themselves to some of the full-fat cream (it just might help them last a little longer on the streets) and everyone else who sat carefully on the three long rows of tables and benches in the little shop he had bought.

Robin had always wanted to open his own "soup" kitchen, and finally after going on some quiz programmes and doing extremely well. He had enough money to open this kitchen on Canterbury high street, and thankfully more and more donations kept pouring in each and every day.

And Robin was still delighted that whenever members of the public came in to give their donations, they were surprised by the rather pleasant smell of the kitchen.

Robin had made sure not to overdo the sweet

scents of oranges, cedarwood and caramel that was sprayed in the kitchen because he still wanted there to be hints of the body odour of the homeless people, but he didn't want the kitchen to smell awful.

It was just right for everyone.

The sound of the homeless people talking, quietly singing and exchanging tips for surviving made Robin happier than he felt like he deserved. He had built his place to help people, and thankfully he was doing that.

"Yo boss man," Robin's sister, Fanny, said as she came up and stood next to him.

Robin was about to speak but sharp pain radiated from his jaw from an old injury. Robin massaged the area for a moment and like every time he just wondered whatever happened to the love of his life. Marcus had been such a sweet, innocent guy.

Robin should have stayed, fought and tried to protect him. But when Marcus' father fractured Robin's jaw, he just knew he had to get out of there.

Now he wished he hadn't.

"Still playing up Ro?" Fanny asked.

Robin smiled at a veteran who gestured to the bread.

"Take as much as you want Francis," Robin said, smiling.

"Bro come on. You need to get back out in the dating market. Any guy would be lucky to have you,"

Robin smiled. He supposed it was true, but the only guy who Robin wanted to have him was Marcus.

Something was that never going to happen.

A crash of thunder echoed around the soup kitchen and Robin felt his stomach tighten.

"I hope everyone else is okay. I wouldn't want the others to be in this storm," Robin said.

Fanny just rolled her eyes as he went to check on everyone. Robin knew she didn't always approve of his constant worry about all the regulars of the soup kitchen, but Robin just wanted to protect them.

Like he should have done for Marcus.

Robin heard the door to the kitchen open as a scarily thin wearing a dirty old hoody, jeans and very holey shoes came in dripping wet.

Robin came out from the counter and went towards the poor homeless man.

But when the guy dropped his hood, Robin couldn't believe how thin and rugged his beard was. Yet the man did… look quite attractive.

Robin could see how this attractive man could have once been a great athlete with a handsome face, broad shoulders and maybe some muscles. And those eyes… those bright blue eyes were amazing.

And Robin couldn't deny the homeless man's long awfully messy brown hair was even a little hot. Robin didn't know why but he felt such a strong attraction and connection to him.

He just didn't know why.

The homeless man tried to smile at Robin and he took a step forward.

Collapsing to the ground from hungry.

Robin rushed forward.

The hot man was unconscious.

***

Marcus woke up a few hours later, his body heavy and feeling awful of fatigue, hungry and something else that he couldn't quite figure out yet. He didn't know where he was, but he just stared weakly up at the bright white ceiling.

Marcus felt something soft and comfortable under him and when he looked at his hand, he was surprised to see an IV line had been put in there. He didn't how he got there but for some reason he was pleased he was okay.

He had just felt so tired, hungry and weak when he walked into the soup kitchen that he tried as best as he could to remain strong, but that was clearly doomed to failure.

But Marcus really hoped that he wasn't dreaming about a tall sexy man with well-styled blond hair wearing a thick blue shirt over his fit body with a little white t-shirt underneath. Marcus didn't know where he knew the look from but he was really turned-on by it. The man looked so perfect.

Marcus forced himself to sit up on the sofa and he saw a large cup of full-milk hot chocolate on the white coffee table in front of him along with five bars of chocolate. There was a little note as well and Marcus couldn't understand why but he felt like he recognised the handwriting.

It was a happy note suggesting Marcus should eat

the chocolate to get some energy and fat back into his body.

After being starving and hungry for so long, Marcus didn't know how his body would take the fat. But it wasn't exactly like he had much of a choice, so he opened one of the chocolate bars and just had to smile.

The chocolate bar was flavoured salted caramel. It was his absolute favourite flavour in the entire world.

Marcus had a feeling that he was going to enjoy it here. A lot.

Then as much as Marcus didn't want to leave, he knew sooner or later he would have to go back out on the streets, and start the whole stupid process of starvation all over again.

Sure, people always believed there was so much support for homeless people. There wasn't. There was what he called "pretend support" where the local councils and governments just wanted to look like they were doing something.

In reality. They were doing nothing.

"You're awake. That's great!" a tall woman said as she came over to Marcus.

He couldn't place her but he felt like he knew her. He felt like he had met her bubbly energy, happiness and passion for helping others before.

"Do I know you?" Marcus asked.

The woman shrugged. "Sorry. I might have treated you before but I don't know. I'm the unofficial doctor of the soup kitchen. I'm a paramedic by trade,"

Marcus smiled. "Thanks for the IV. I used to know a trainee paramedic a few months ago, she went to a local uni,"

The woman sat down next to him and smiled.

"Maybe I know her. Tell me her name," she said.

Marcus's eyebrows rose. He had struggled to remember it for a few moments, then he smiled.

"Fanny Ossam," Marcus said. "Do you know her?"

The woman looked shocked. Then she looked Marcus up and down like she was inspecting him.

He remembered a woman doing that before.

"Are you her?" Marcus asked.

"And are you Marcus?" she asked.

Marcus smiled and started laughing. He didn't know how to react to all this good news. He was finally getting a chance to see this great wonderful woman again, a woman who wanted to give the world so much love, medical help and passion.

But where was Robin?

Marcus gently took her hands but he quickly realised how strange it felt. His hands were basically skin and bone at his point, unlike hers.

"Robin?" Marcus asked.

Fanny smiled briefly and pointed to the chocolate.

"I'll go and get him if you want. I would just eat and drink all the chocolate," she said.

Marcus felt his hands turn sweaty and hot. He was actually going to see the love of his life again, he didn't know how to take it.

He nodded. Fanny quickly went over to get her brother.

Marcus couldn't believe this was happening and that just made him more and more excited.

***

Robin forced himself not to hiss in pain as he felt his stomach tighten more and more as he wondered if the hot guy upstairs on his sofa was going to be okay. He was so hot and beautiful and wonderful (even in his condition) that Robin seriously wanted him to be okay.

Even though he had literally just met him, Robin felt so connected and in lust over him. Robin had made sure he was comfortable, okay and had all the needed medical stuff that he needed to survive.

He had even given the hot man some high-calorie paste and that was normally sent out to Africa to give to starving children there. That was how bad the hot man was.

Robin heard the light footsteps of Fanny walk up to him as he continued to stand at the counter with new piping hot containers of soup, cream and bread for the evening crowd of homeless people.

Sadly because all of the rain earlier, the temperature had dropped so it was mostly ice now. He just hoped that no one was injured.

"Ro," Fanny said concerned.

"What is it? Is the man dead?" Robin asked.

Fanny weakly smiled. "That man. It's Marcus,"

Robin shrugged. "Marcus who? And why do you act like I know him? The guy's hot but I've not-"

Fanny carefully tapped the side of Robin's jaw where Marcus's father had fractured it only a few months before.

His eyes widened and he felt like he was going to collapse. He had never expected this and Robin was such a failure.

All Robin had ever wanted to do was love, protect and be with Marcus. Clearly that had failed in spectacular fashion, as the love of his life was now homeless and starving and so close to death if he hadn't of arrived at the kitchen when he did.

"I'll keep an eye out here," Fanny said, slightly pushing Robin to go upstairs.

He slowly nodded and went upstairs into his large apartment above the kitchen. He loved the large floor-to-ceiling windows that made the apartment feel so big and spacious.

Then Robin saw the homeless remains of Marcus and he really did see it.

That was the reason why he felt so connected and passionate and saw the potential of this hot sexy guy. Because he had been in love with him for so long.

Robin went over to the sofa and sat carefully next to Marcus who looked like he was going to be sick after eating all the chocolate.

Robin just wrapped his arms round him.

"I'm sorry," Robin said, fighting back the tears.

He was expecting himself to feel happiness or relief that he was finally reunited with his love, but in that moment he only felt crippling guilt.

Marcus wrapped his arms around Robin, and Robin had to admit it felt so strange having someone this thin love you.

Then Marcus's little fingers raised Robin's chin, and Robin just loved staring into those amazing dark blue eyes. This was definitely Marcus, the man he loved.

Marcus slowly ran his fingers up Robin's jaw. Robin hissed and pulled away slightly.

"I'm sorry. What's wrong?" Marcus asked.

Robin honestly didn't know how to tell his love this, but he was just going to have to.

"I never wanted to leave you that day. I never wanted this to happen to you. Your father fractured my jaw so I ran," Robin said.

Marcus took a large sigh and Robin felt him wrap his hand around the back of his neck.

Marcus pulled him close and kissed him. Robin hadn't felt another man's lips for so long. They felt amazing.

"I don't care about the past," Marcus said. "My ex-family were dicks. But what happens now?"

Robin wondered for a moment if he was talking about any hints of getting back together, but as he sat there savouring the surprising softness of Marcus's lips, it was like they had never been a part.

But Robin sadly knew that he wasn't talking as a potential boyfriend.

He was talking as a homeless person.

Robin hated having this conversation with any homeless person. The conversation that made the soup kitchen seem so pointless. Because the soup kitchen wasn't a large enough charity yet, they didn't have any bedrooms or outreach programmes to help the homeless people get work and build new lives.

So at the end of every day, Robin had to send them back out into the cold. It seemed so pointless but that was how the UK local governments worked. They didn't care about homelessness, so there were barely any grants to apply for to get some extra money to help set up these programmes.

But Marcus wasn't just a homeless person.

Robin gently ran his fingers through Marcus's hair and kissed him again and again.

"I love you Marcus," he said. "And I never want to be a part from you again. Will you stay with me?"

Marcus looked around, laughed and kissed Robin harder than he ever had before.

And Robin loved it.

***

A few months later, Marcus was laying again on the amazing softness of Robin's sofa with his head resting on Robin's lap as they talked, laughed and made up for a lot of lost time.

Marcus loved the wonderful smell of the herbs,

freshly baked breads and warming soup that he had made today. And after teaching some life skill classes to some other homeless people, Marcus just felt amazing.

He was thankfully back to his normal weight and Marcus loved it how Robin would explore his body at night. Most of the time Robin was just in so much lust, Marcus didn't know what Robin was doing. But for Marcus having Robin exploring him so much, just felt so strange after being so skinny for so long.

But it made him feel the best he had ever felt. He loved it.

As Robin spoke about his plans for the future and got Marcus' ideas on it as they were both co-owners (with Fanny as the official part-time paramedic) of the soup kitchen, Marcus kept playing with the large engagement ring on his finger, and he couldn't admit how much he loved these nights.

The delightful nights that were always filled with love, affection and talking. Sure, something the talking was just about the business and the charity, but sometimes it was so much more intimate and special.

At the end of all this terribleness of the past year, Marcus was so glad that Robin had given him what his family never could.

Love, attention and respect.

And as Marcus looked more and more forward to the wedding next year, Marcus vowed to help and protect every single homeless person who walked through their doors.

GAY SWEET ROMANCE COLLECTION

COLD DECEMBER NIGHT

Gabe Turner absolutely loved the month of December. You had the Christmas parties, the gifts and spending time with the family on Christmas day. That was honestly his most favourite thing of the month, sitting round the large dinner table surrounded by plenty of great juicy, succulent food that was mouth-watering.

It was Gabe's idea of heaven.

Except he did hate how dark it got in December. It got dark so early that every single day of the week, Gabe would have to drive to work and back home in the pitch black.

Now Gabe was never the sort of man to be scared of driving in the dark. That wasn't him in the slightest, but in the month of December he always seemed to have some kind of accident when driving. Two years ago, he had hit another parked car that was as black as the darkness.

Last year, he had crashed into someone's wall

because a deer shot out in front of him. Gabe seriously didn't want to know what would happen this year.

In fact Gabe was actually even more nervous tonight than usual because he was driving back from a massive superstore up in London because his mother apparently just had to have the brand new turkey joint they specialised in. Apparently it was from a special farm in Italy and whatnot and fed with Italian stuff and yea... Gabe didn't really care.

And with him being the good son he was, he went to get it straight away after work.

Gabe drove down a very narrow country lane with massive bendy twisted oaks lining the road. Its long menacing branches reaching out in all directions in some unsubtle attempt to grab some prey driving past.

The sooner Gabe got out of this place the better, it seemed he had taken a wrong turn somewhere and to his annoyance his Sat-nav refused to work and clearly someone was about to go wrong.

Gabe felt the freezing icy cold of the December night invade his car and his breath was slowly starting to turn more and more solid. Gabe was starting to get concerned about his windscreen steaming up too much.

The road rather sharply bent to the left and Gabe drove round it.

Gabe bravely opened his car window to stop the warmth of his car from condensing on the windscreen anymore than it already was. The last thing he needed or wanted was to be blinded on this dangerous narrow road.

As the icy cold air blasted into the car, Gabe was met with the strong scents of dampness, refreshing nature and the subtle smell of his burnt clutch. Because Gabe had been an awful driver earlier than really damaged his clutch by staying in too low a gear for too long.

The very last thing he needed before Christmas was his clutch to go. He didn't want that, he certainly didn't have the money for it.

That was one of the bad things about working in a bank, having a great sweet boyfriend that apparently loved you so much, only to have him learn your passwords and steal a bunch of your money.

And to make matters even worse that same ex-boyfriend dared to take out a credit card in your name and max it out all before Gabe realised what was happening.

As much as Gabe just knew that the vast, vast majority of hot sexy men weren't like that, it still pained him a lot.

But he had never had much luck with men and at the age of 25 Gabe was starting to think mainstream gay culture might be on to something. Maybe constant hook-ups were the way to go.

Plenty of fun without the commitment.

Gabe just smiled and shook his head at that silly idea. Gabe had actually tried a few hook-ups back at university and they were great, fun and exciting but they always left him wanting more connection with the other guy. Even those that defeated the point of hook-ups with no strings attached.

The road shot round to the right. Gabe turned.

Thankfully he managed to drive safely enough that he didn't crash or come off the road but this was just dangerous now.

The smell of Gabe's burnt clutch got a lot worse and Gabe saw the edge of his bonnet glow red, so Gabe slowly pulled over, popped out and went to check out what was going on.

Gabe coughed as he shone his phone's flashlight into the engine compartment and because one of his old straight crushes was a mechanic. He quickly realised that his clutch was dead.

As dead as a doornail.

Gabe swore under his breath as his car was now damaged and unusable, and to make matters tons worse he didn't have any phone service to call for a breakdown recovery vehicle to help him out.

Gabe looked around and realised he was in the middle of nowhere on an icy cold December night with not another soul within miles. Gabe was just standing there in the eerily icy silence.

If this was a horror story then Gabe knew he would most probably be killed in the next few moments.

But he had to try to get some help somewhere.

So he put on his spare gloves and hats that he

always carried in the boot, locked his car up tight and set off in the direction he had been driving on foot.

He just hoped he could find someone to help him.

***

Looking after his parents' little farmhouse on their little plot of land in the middle of absolutely nowhere was definitely not Leon Saxon's first idea of a fun evening. Normally, Leon would be dancing, kissing and meeting plenty of great wonderful guys in the local clubs and bars around his university's city.

But that clearly wasn't going to happen for a little while with him coming home for the Christmas Holidays and his boyfriend dumping him. All because apparently Leon wasn't suitable for meeting his parents and seeing them over Christmas.

Leon just found it flat out funny. So what if he enjoyed living life, enjoying himself and being rather active in the bedroom department?

It definitely didn't make him a bad boyfriend, but when Leon's parents said they were going to mainland Europe for a long weekend and needed someone to watch the farmhouse for them. Leon jumped at the chance because it was free and even though he would never ever admit it, there was a rather rustic charm to the place.

Leon laid on the long brown sofa in the middle of the very large living room with its cream white walls, large rustic oak beams and wonderfully decorated floor. To anyone else the floor was probably just hardwood to them, but to Leon, he loved the large fake fur rug that was absolutely perfect for making love on.

Not that he had ever done that of course.

Leon also loved the immense fireplace that was build straight in the heart of the living room and he set it up earlier. The weather outside was far, far too cold and icy not to have it on. Leon was just glad he was in here and not outside.

As Leon listened to the crackling, popping and hissing of the logs as their breathtaking flames danced in the fireplace. Leon just stared up at the pure white ceiling with his hands behind his head and just relaxed.

His parents might have had all the latest entertainment systems, movies and streaming services in the living room, but he just didn't want to do that.

He supposed in a strange way he was still a little heartbroken over the breakup, and being called unworthy to meet his ex's family.

When someone else mentioned it, Leon would naturally say that the ex was dull, boring and moany anything so it didn't really matter. But deep down it really did. Leon had been with him for so long and he just felt strange and like he was missing a part of himself.

Like tonight, Leon would much rather be talking, laughing and loving his ex compared to being stuck here by himself in the freezing cold with only a roaring fire to keep him company.

The subtle smells of wood smoke, burning pine and burning sap left the great, but strange, taste of family barbeques on his tongue. They were certainly simpler times before he knew he was gay, loved partying and living life.

Knowing that he couldn't just lay here all night, Leon decided he probably should watch a film. Maybe a gay romance one (given how few there sadly were), maybe a fantasy film so he could escape, or maybe he would just lay here a little longer.

Someone knocked on the door.

Leon had absolutely no clue who the hell would be out in the middle of nowhere on this icy night and actually want to come in. It was probably just the wind knocking something over so Leon kept laying on the sofa.

The knocking was a lot harder.

The knocking was probably just a sad lonely person who wanted to rob him or something. If Leon didn't pay attention the creep would probably leave him alone sooner or later.

"Hello! Is anyone in there! My car's broken down and I need to call a recovery van. Please!"

Leon grinned slightly at the sound of the man's voice. There was something… sexy and manly about it. It was deep, young and rather velvety. It was so different to the rather more high-pitched voice of his ex that maybe this sexy voice could help distract him for a little while.

After all he didn't have something better to do.

Leon slowly got up from the sofa, walked through a long corridor that jetted out from the living door and towards the farm house's large black door.

He opened it and... shit!

Leon felt his knees were about to buckle as he looked at the fucking beautiful man standing in front of him. The man was clearly freezing cold but in his thick blue hat that seriously bought out the colour of his eyes, his tight thick coat that really highlighted his fit body and his black glasses that seriously framed his entire face perfectly.

Wow! This guy was perfection!

Leon just knew his night was going to get a lot better!

***

Out of everything Gabe had been expecting as he walked through the bitter cold countryside for over an hour, been attacked by tons of branches and almost got run over by a young idiot. Gabe never expected to run across a little farm in the middle of nowhere.

Gabe had really liked the four large fields with the wonderful farmhouse in the centre. There was something so rustic and charming and delightful about it all.

But Gabe was definitely a lot more interested in the outrageously handsome man in front of him.

Gabe just couldn't understand why there was such a sweet sexy man in front of him, wearing nothing but a loose fitting white top, black jeans and short dirty blond hair. This man was just so gorgeous and stunning and his body... Gabe could just tell from the looseness of his top how fit he was.

Hot Man gestured Gabe to come in and he wasn't going to say no. Then the Hot Man led Gabe into the living room which Gabe was flat out stunned by.

From the outside he never would have known that the living room was so large inside. And the cream white walls, large brown sofa and the hardwood floors were great.

In fact, Gabe had to focus on the little cuts and veins and streaks running through the brown hardwood. He had heard of a similar design technique from a friend studying interior design, and whilst it was so hard for a normal person to notice it. The added colour, texture and look given to the hardwood made such a difference.

Gabe looked up at Hot Man again and he was confused to see Hot Man sort of stunned at him.

"You okay?" Gabe asked. "Did I do something wrong?"

Hot Man smiled, and... Gabe felt the need to sit down. Hot Man's smile was seriously starting to melt his legs away.

"No. It's just. No one ever notices the hardwood floors. My parents hate it how no one has a keen enough eye to see them, and before you ask. Yes they are snobby eccentrics when it comes to flooring and design,"

Gabe felt so stupid compared to this Hot Man. He felt like each word this amazing man was saying just dumbed him down.

Gabe hated that he was acting like this but he felt like such an innocent schoolboy next to this Hot Man.

Hot Man came over to Gabe and Gabe touched his arm to steady himself. Hot Man's strong earthy aftershave made Gabe's heart race, blood rushed to his wayward parts and Hot Man just smelt amazing.

Even the pure chemistry Gabe felt between them as he touched his arm was electrical. Clearly Hot Man was feeling the same as he gently led Gabe to the sofa and they both sat down close to each other.

A lot closer than strangers or even friends would sit together.

"Um," Gabe said, trying to force out words in front of this hot sexy man. "I'm Gabe and can I use your telephone please?"

Hot Man smiled. Gabe felt like such an idiot, what young person uses the word *telephone* anymore?

Gabe needed to concentrate a lot more and get his act together.

"I'm Leon and yea you can use my phone," Hot Man said as he gave Gabe his smartphone.

Gabe quickly called the recovery people, told him the rough location of his car and they sadly told him they wouldn't be able to get there for a few hours.

Then Leon took the phone off him and told the recovery people that Gabe would be staying at a farmhouse on the stretch of road for a little while. Gabe was actually surprised at the delight that the recovery person sounded at that news.

Leon hung up and smiled at Gabe. "The Recovery People said they'll stop here on the way and then they'll drive you to your car,"

Gabe was very glad about that. The last thing he wanted was to walk back at in the freezing cold again, and Gabe knew it was only going to get colder and colder.

"And you're okay about me staying here for a while?" Gabe asked.

Leon gave him such a boyish grin. "Of course. I wouldn't offer if I didn't mean it,"

Gabe couldn't help but grin too. He tried not to, but the idea of spending a few hours with this hot sexy man just made his trousers strain a little.

And judging by the smile on Leon's face he felt the exact same way.

***

Over the next few hours Leon couldn't believe how much he had embarrassed himself. He had snorted when he laughed, he had confessed things to Gabe that he wouldn't to anyone else and he just couldn't believe how relaxed he felt around him.

Leon and Gabe were laying on the sofa together and Leon seriously loved feeling Gabe's body heat against him, and… this was just heaven.

For the past few hours, they had done literally nothing but talk, laugh and tell each other everything.

Leon had told Gabe about his ex and that had lead to the vast conversations (and very deep ones) about love, relationships and the future.

Leon had hung on Gabe's every single little word as they both drank some hot chocolate Leon had made and found in his parents' cupboards. It was the very, very good stuff that they had bought back from one of their many travels to the continent that the entire family loved so much- mainland Europe.

Leon had helped Gabe to clean up his hot chocolate moustache, and Gabe had helped him clear up when Leon had spilt some of his.

And never during the past few hours had either of them checked the time, wanted to watch TV or look at their phones. Leon was just obsessed with talking and looking at this fucking hot guy in front of him.

Leon had no idea how lucky he was to at least get these past few hours with such a wonderful man who made him laugh, smile and feel the most alive he had in weeks (and probably ever).

But when there was a knock at the door, Leon felt his heart sink like the titanic and he just knew that this night of amazing fun was over.

His insanely hot Gabe would have to leave him, get his car fixed and he would probably never see him again.

And that just flat out killed him inside.

As much as both the men looked at each other with boyish grins, wide eyes and smile lines breaking up their faces. They both knew that this was probably goodbye.

Leon wanted to ask Gabe to call him, come and see him again or at least exchange phone numbers. But he was scared. He was scared of getting hurt again and he wasn't sure if this night was what he wanted to turn into a relationship.

Wasn't it better at the end of the day to remember an amazing night? Compared to a long dull relationship that would end in tears and heartbreak?

Leon knew that was just the fear talking, but as he opened the front door and watched the recovery woman in her bright orange uniform talk to Gabe. Leon just couldn't help but feel his heart sink even more.

Before the recovery woman and Gabe left, Gabe tried to lean in for a kiss but Leon stupidly leant away and hugged him instead.

After the pain of the last breakup, Leon just didn't know if he could do it again. And it was only now he was finally realising how much damage that breakup and putting told he was unworthy was affecting him.

And as Leon watched the recovery vehicle drive away he just knew he had made a massive mistake.

The worse mistake of his life.

One he didn't know how to fix.

***

"Thank you!" Gabe shouted as he watched the massive recovery vehicle drive away and the words condensed in the bitterly cold air in front of him.

The air was the coldest Gabe had ever felt and as he got into his little icy cold black car, Gabe just sat there for a few moments.

He had had such an amazing, sexy and delightful evening that he never wanted it to end. He wanted to get to know Leon even more, kiss him and just... just be boyfriends with him.

It felt so silly after only meeting and spending an evening and night with him, but Gabe felt like there was such a strong intimate connection between them. Gabe had absolutely loved laying on the sofa with Leon.

He had loved everything about tonight.

When he had been with past boyfriends or hook-ups (the very few there were), Gabe had always ended up looking at his phone, watching TV or doing something that took the focus away from his boyfriend.

That was simply impossible to do tonight.

But clearly this was just a night of fun and interest and sexual tension to Leon. Clearly he didn't want anything more or he would have said something and he certainly would have let Gabe kiss him.

Then again maybe Gabe should have said something. Maybe he should have asked for his phone number, asked if he could spend the night there properly and slept there, maybe he should have done a lot.

As Gabe turned on his car, it was crystal clear

that him and Leon weren't meant to be together and the fates or whatever determined love was equally determined not to have them together. So why fight it?

Gabe cocked his head at that strange idea. He really enjoyed and probably loved Leon so it was only right that Gabe at least asked him point blank if Leon felt the same way about him.

Gabe had to talk to Leon one last time.

So Gabe started driving up the dangerously narrow awful country trees and his stomach filled with butterflies at the idea of asking Leon out on a proper date.

Gabe was coming up to a corner when a little silver car shot round, almost crashed into Gabe and then braked hard.

Gabe stopped too and just couldn't believe how silly this driver was. He was going to have to shout at him because he was going to get himself or another driver killed.

The silver car door opened and Gabe felt his throat close up as he stared at the stunning beauty of Leon standing there in his thin white top, shivering cold.

It was so cute seeing Leon and his teeth chattering away.

Gabe immediately went over to him and wrapped his coat around this stunning beautiful man freezing in front of him.

"I was just coming to see you. What are you

doing?" Gabe said, looking into Leon's seductively stunning eyes.

Leon tried a schoolboy grin but his teeth were chattering too much.

"I had to see you. Don't go away. I-"

Before Leon could say anymore, Gabe had to kiss him. The softness and taste of Leon's amazing lips were so perfect and the sheer love and power and chemistry that flood both of them was immense.

The two men stood there in the middle of the road, staring into each other's eyes, holding each other close on that cold December night.

"I'm not going anywhere if you don't want me to," Gabe said.

Leon's eyes wettened and they both kissed again. Then without saying a word to each other, they both got in their cars and started to drive back to the farmhouse.

Gabe couldn't believe how perfect and excited he was that this was happening. This was going to be a perfect night and Gabe already knew exactly what he was going to get Leon for Christmas. Something that would mean the world to beautiful Leon.

He was going to introduce him to his family on Christmas day when he took the specialise turkey that had caused this amazing night round to his parents.

Not because this was a whirlwind romance, but because Gabe knew deep, deep down that this was right, perfect and Leon was the last person he would ever think of as unworthy of anything.

And to Gabe, that was definitely the definition of true love.

DRIVING HOME FOR LOVE

Adam O'Dell was driving along a rather wonderful stretch of an English three-laned motorway (if such a thing was possible), plenty of snow covered pine trees lining the motorway and thankfully no other driver was on the road.

He liked that on Christmas day because it meant that everyone was safely with their families, laughing and enjoying themselves.

Adam did like the delightful smell of the damp pine that filled the car as he drove down the motorway and the trees outside were giving off their wonderful scents. And strangely enough it reminded him of great family holidays in the breath-taking forests of Sweden as a child, and those famous meaty, juicy Swedish meatballs that Adam absolutely loved.

But with large snowflakes starting to rain down on the motorway, Adam was seriously starting to wish he had listened to his parent's advice of driving up to their Christmas Eve so he could spend the night with them and his siblings.

Adam hated it when they were right.

Adam had plenty of presents, cards and decorations that he had picked up on his travels around the wonderful Christmas markets of mainland Europe. Adam loved each and one of them because unlike the cold commercial ones of the UK, the real European ones had such amazing character, personality and Christmas spirit that had seemed to die out long ago here.

Or maybe that was just Adam.

He had wanted to bring a guy back to his loving family for Christmas for years now and he was so sure he was going to get a guy this year. That never happened and now Adam was driving back alone in the freezing cold.

He knew that his loving family wouldn't mind but he didn't want yet another year of being surrounded by his mum, dad and his siblings each with their own amazing partner and lover. Adam wanted to be included, he wanted to love, celebrate and be with someone at this special time of year.

Adam wanted to bring someone back for Christmas more than anything else in the world.

His breath started to condense in front of his eyes as he kept driving down the motorway and visibility was dropping.

Adam just wanted to get to his parents' house over sixty miles away, hug his family and hear about their latest jobs, travels and other adventures.

That was something he really loved about his family. Even though they all had so-called "mundane" jobs. Everyone in his family always had a story to tell, and Adam was seriously looking forward to telling them his story about travelling through mainland Europe in his car and getting lost plenty of times on the way.

Most people in the UK probably wouldn't find that very fun at all, but Adam loved that his family would. They would all probably laugh, joke and compare it to the stories that the others had.

Adam really, really wanted to win their unofficial competition about who had the best story for Christmas. Adam didn't know what the others were doing or how good their stories were, but he just hoped his travels were great enough.

The sound of hail gently tapping on his car made Adam roll his eyes at the bad weather. This was the last thing he needed, he just needed the weather to behave for a little while longer and then the weather could do whatever it wanted.

Being snowed in at his parents' house with his siblings would hardly be a bad thing until the new year, but Adam had to get there first.

At this point normal people might have made the petal hit the floor but Adam was definitely not that dangerous. He was going to keep driving safely no matter what.

Smoke poured out of his engine.

Adam's eyes widened.

He quickly pulled over on the hard shoulder, grabbed his phone and got out of his car.

Adam opened up the bonnet and hissed as tons of steam, smoke and liquid poured out of the engine.

"Damn," Adam muttered.

He seriously didn't need this. He just wanted to be with family on this most special of days, but oh no, the world had other plans for him.

He just didn't know in what delightful ways yet.

***

Mechanic Arthur Smith absolutely hated working on Christmas day. In fact he slightly hated the entire Christmas season, his family had disowned him at the age of twenty-one, he had no boyfriend and a very shitty job that he wasn't too keen on.

Arthur had wanted to join the Royal Navy the second he turned eighteen, but they took one look at him, realised he was gay and they made up tons of excuses why he couldn't be enrolled.

Their lost.

Arthur drove down a massive horrible stretch of motorway with foul pine trees lining it and the disgusting smell of damp pine filled his van as he drove. Arthur didn't want to have to smell that rubbish, he wanted to smell the amazing scents of a man, but that was clearly never going to happen.

As much as Arthur just wanted to enjoy Christmas with some friends, maybe a boyfriend (if he could get one) and relax. He hated the reality of his life and that those desires or dreams were just never going to happen.

Especially as he was stuck in a job that made him work antisocial hours and it made him work Christmas Day.

And as for the people who dared to drive on Christmas Day, they were just stupid. Everyone should travel up to their parents', friends' or wherever they're going before the big day. It was just silly to drive on Christmas day.

Arthur was going to tell the idiot he was driving to see now. The idiot must have seen the bad weather warning on the forecasts recently, but this idiot was probably just arrogant enough that he thought he could win against the weather.

Idiot!

As Arthur kept driving with the snowflakes getting larger and larger, he couldn't believe how bad this was, and he wasn't sure how he was going to do this job.

He doubted he was going to be able to see the engine, the car and the person. So he might just have to wait until the weather cleared up. Mainly because it was too risky to call in a flat-bed lorry to take the car away (and it didn't help that none of its drivers were on shift).

After a few more moments of driving, Arthur noticed a large orange light in the distance and he rolled his eyes as he had finally arrived at his job.

He pulled over in the hard shoulder and shook his head even more at all the smoke, steam and liquid that was coming off the car. Most people driving past (of which there were none) probably would have imagined it was the snow or hail or something.

Yet Arthur knew the damage was bad and he would probably need to fix the engine with equipment back at the mechanic shop. He really didn't want that.

Arthur put on his gloves, thick coat and hat before he climbed out of his van and went towards the little car. That was another stupid thing about this idiot, a little car like this was never going to be able to survive in these conditions.

But Arthur couldn't see the driver.

He thankfully didn't see anyone outside the car, so Arthur went over to the passenger side of the car, tapped on a window and a click happened.

Arthur took that as a sign he should get in. He did.

Arthur got in the small car and was about to yell and give the idiot driver a piece of his mind when he… when he actually looked at the amazing man next to him.

There was just something so handsome, alluring and seductive about the man's smooth young face, well-styled young hair and hot-as-hell overcoat.

Arthur hadn't realised until now but he really had a thing for men in overcoats, or maybe it was just this man.

Within moments he felt like he was a schoolboy again unsure of how to act, talk or look in front of such a stunning man. Should he extend his hand, hug the man or just be nice?

Be nice.

"You from the recovery people?" the hot blond man asked.

Arthur forced his head to move but he didn't want to lose sight of the hot man. And even with the biting chill of the air outside seeping into the car, Arthur struggled to hide how hot he was inside.

He feared he might actually start sweating.

"Yea. I'm Arthur," he said.

The hot man smiled and turned away from Arthur. He didn't know how to take that, but he was here to do a job first and foremost.

"Adam," the hot man said.

Adam was a very hot name. Arthur really wanted to talk more and learn more about this stunningly hot man but he at least needed to pretend to work.

"Let's see what the problem is," Arthur said gesturing they should get out of the car.

And Arthur so badly wanted to add, if Adam got cold. The two of them could easily warm up in his van.

***

After meeting such an outrageous gorgeous guy, Adam had no clue what to do with himself. He had had to look away from the guy in the car just so he didn't make a weird sound, kiss him or just do anything to embarrass himself.

Adam had been waiting so long in his car when

the gorgeous guy turned up that he didn't know what to do with himself.

He just loved Arthur's slight beard, manly looking working clothes and his young handsome face. There was something so youthful about him but it was like he had so much experience too. He might also be into travelling, Adam would seriously love that.

He would love a wonderfully hot guy to travel with, work with and get to spend Christmas with him.

As the two men stood in front of the smoking, steaming and spitting engine, Adam had no idea what he was looking at. All he knew about engines was it was what powered the car to move him from A to B.

That was it.

But the amazing thing was Arthur looked like he was inspecting some sort of grand masterpiece and feat of engineering. His eyes were so focused on each part of the engine and car that Adam couldn't even begin to understand what he was so interested in.

Thankfully the biting cold, howling wind and the snow had stopped enough that Arthur was able to examine the car properly.

Adam started shivering more and more as he just stood there whilst Arthur did whatever he was doing. His teeth were chattering and he just wanted to do something to keep himself warm.

Arthur stood up and looked at Adam. His face twisted into some kind of fear, and as much as Adam just wanted his concern to be about his safety. He sadly knew Arthur was being professional.

Sadly.

Arthur wrapped a massively strong arm round Adam's shoulders, and Adam failed to keep his wayward parts of getting excited. Adam flat out loved the wonderful chemistry, power and electricity that flowed between them.

"You can wait in my van if you want. It's perfectly warm," Arthur said.

Adam wanted to stay out here and look at Arthur's amazing ass as he bent over to work on his car, but he was cold. And his mother would kill him if he turned up ill or something.

Adam slowly nodded and Arthur guided him over to his van and placed Adam on the front seat.

What really surprised Adam was how sad Arthur looked as he shut the door and went back over to work on his car. And Adam felt the same, he might have just met Arthur twenty minutes ago but he felt almost connected to him in some strange way.

Adam moved his knees and accidentally opened the glove compartment, and seriously smiled as plenty of small travel leaflets fell out.

This insanely hot guy was also into travelling, adventures and having fun.

Now Adam was really, really looking forward to when he came back.

***

Arthur couldn't understand why he was finding this particular job so tortuous and hard. Normally he loved all mechanical jobs and working on cars, but this one felt strange.

It did not feel boring per se, but the job didn't feel as exciting as it normally did when Arthur finished up a car.

He had tapped, hammered and replaced some of the pieces of the engine and fixed a bunch of stuff that should have been picked up in an MOT. But the car would soon be all perfectly fixed up.

Arthur just needed to refill the engine's oil, coolant and power steering as he had needed to drain it earlier in order to fix the car. That had been thankfully a clean job compared to normal.

Arthur felt his stomach fill with butterflies as he went back over to his van and saw Adam doing something, or at least looking at something.

He opened the side door of the van, climbed in and went to find the liquid he needed.

"You like travel?" Adam asked.

Arthur shrugged, knowing he had found his travel leaflets.

"Yea. Me and my family use to go twice a year to different places. My family could always find a great deal and go there cheap," Arthur said.

"Definitely. My parents are the same. Are you going there today?"

Arthur went silent. He didn't want to explain this beautiful sexy man how his parents had abandoned him and kicked him out a few years ago to this day.

"Oh," Adam said. "I'm sorry,"

Arthur shrugged again. "It's in the past. What are your parents like?"

"They're great. Me and my siblings always get together at Christmas no matter where we are in the world,"

Arthur looked at him and so badly wanted to kiss this sexy man as he saw Adam's face resting on his seats and his blond hair lightly falling over his eyes.

Damn this guy was cute.

"You sound like a travelled family," Arthur forced out. He was too focused on Adam's beauty.

"Yes. I tend to work in mainland Europe a lot. My sisters work in Japan, Australia and New Zealand and my brother works in America,"

Arthur flat out didn't know what to say, how the hell could he compete with his family?

Adam and the rest of his family clearly had some kind of amazing jobs. How was a mere lonely mechanic meant to fit in with all that?

He probably wasn't.

"Do you have any Christmas plans?" Adam asked, seductively.

Arthur didn't dare look at Adam as he asked that. He didn't want to be completely disarmed of his logic by his beauty.

Arthur shook his head.

"Then you need to come back to ours. Hear the story of our travels and I want to hear more about you," Adam asked.

Arthur didn't know what to say.

He panicked, grabbed the liquid he needed and ran out of the van.

***

Adam's heart felt like a solid rock inside him as he watched Arthur hurry back over to his car and start to fill it. All Adam had wanted was to spend a day and hopefully longer with this hot beautiful guy that made him feel hot, sweaty and ever so young again.

Maybe he was too forceful, maybe he was too pushy, maybe Arthur wasn't interested in him whatsoever.

Adam had been so sure about Arthur and they both felt about each other. But it wouldn't have been the first time he had been so wrong about a beautiful guy. Maybe this was all just some kind of marketing tactic that the recovery people used to make him feel relaxed and happy with the service.

That was probably it.

At this rate Adam didn't know if he wanted to go to his parents anymore. Seeing his mum and dad deeply in love after thirty years of marriage and then seeing his siblings and their partners would just be some kind of evil torture.

And Adam would certainly be jealous of all of their success in the love department whilst Adam had been a complete failure.

Maybe this was going to be the great story he was going to tell his family in some pathetic effort to win the unofficial competition. The story of how he had met, loved and been abandoned by an insanely hot guy.

Well, it was true at the very least.

The smell of damp pine seemed so cold and distant now like even the weather was admitting he was a lost cause, so all Adam wanted to do was leave this awful motorway, force himself to drive to his parents and just fall on the sofa. Or maybe drink the day away so he could forget about how he forced a hot guy to run away from him.

A few moments later someone pounded on the van window and Adam was surprised to see Arthur smiling at him. Adam opened the door and loved the feeling of Arthur's body warmth pressing against him as Arthur moved closer.

"I'm sorry I ran away. I was just unsure. No one has ever offered that to me before," he said.

Adam still wasn't impressed.

"Any chance your parents have room for one more?" Arthur asked, placing his gloved hands on Adam's.

As Adam felt the love and warmth pulsing through them both, Adam couldn't stay mad at Arthur and he somehow just knew that Arthur meant it. He truly did want to spend the day with him, his parents and his siblings.

Maybe it could be the start of something magical, wonderful and something that last until death did them part.

Adam would love that, and he knew Arthur

would too.

Adam didn't answer Arthur with words, he kissed the beautiful sexy man in front of him, and felt the raw power of their budding love explode between them.

Arthur gave Adam such a schoolboy smile and passed him his keys. Adam popped out of the van and Arthur wrapped his strong arms round him for another kiss.

"Follow me," Adam said playfully.

"Always," Arthur said biting his lip.

As Adam went over to his car and started to drive away and saw Arthur was following him, he knew that he was definitely going to tell this story to the rest of his family. Not because it was a story of meeting, falling in love and being abandoned by an insanely hot guy.

But because it was a great story of driving home for love.

GAY SWEET ROMANCE COLLECTION

LOVE AT THE WINTER WEDDING

Sebastian always had the same problems with weddings regardless of whether he was invited, he was a plus-one or if the wedding people were great friends of him. Weddings were rather cruel for people who couldn't find love in the slightest.

A lot of previous ex-boyfriends had called Sebastian a hopeless romantic, and to be honest, he was. Sebastian just loved the amazing power of romance and showing your boyfriend that you loved them.

But as Sebastian placed down the last fork in the massive reception area (fancy word for a very massive tent in the church grounds) with its white walls, rows upon rows of round white tables and head table at the very front. Sebastian just wasn't impressed with them.

He had designed the perfect wedding for his best friend Harrold and his girlfriend Lilly (Sebastian would have loved Harrold to be gay) of five years with the perfect design, menu and music that the couple would love.

But when the happy couple had asked Sebastian who he was bringing to their wedding, he had quickly changed the subject.

That was definitely a serious problem with being an amateur(ish) wedding planner and then turning up to a wedding single. That was not a good look in the slightest and Sebastian hated to admit it but it had cost him a job or two.

It was completely ridiculous to Sebastian, he had trained for years as a wedding planner as an apprentice to one of the best in London. He knew his stuff about weddings like the back of his hands, but for starters, not too many people wanted a gay planner, and even less of them wanted a single planner.

Sebastian just smiled when he heard the fears of would-be brides that a gay wedding planner would "corrupt" their husbands-to-be and it would ruin the wedding.

Well. That had only happened once and the husband-to-be was gay anyway just marrying to get his parents off his back. It was hardly Sebastian's fault.

Sebastian loved the wonderful smells of lavender, cedarwood and something akin to earthy sexy aftershave that filled the reception area. Sooner or later the wedding would be finished in the Church and then the wedding party would come here.

Sebastian couldn't believe how excited he was

about it. He loved seeing people make toasts, sing and dance together to celebrate the happy couple. It was one of the highlights of being a wedding planner and best friends with the very hot groom.

The distance sound of the organ playing in the church made Sebastian focus on every little detail of the reception area. He went round making sure every linen napkin was straight, every fork, knife and spoon was spotless and most importantly there was more than enough champagne for the couple.

Sebastian had spoken to an extremely cute waiter early about the situation and the entire kitchen staff was aware of the alcohol needs of the happy couple's parents, friends and family.

Apparently the happy couple only drank champagne so it was the other guests that needed to be the focus of the wait staff.

And thankfully the kitchen staff had no problems making the delightful menu of golden crispy chicken goujons, succulent pork medallion in a delicious red wine sauce and the sweetest, creamiest chocolate lava cake for dessert.

Sebastian just hoped that everything would run perfectly smoothly and in an ideal world he would just have a chance to relax tonight. The couple had the reception area until midnight which was seven hours away, and as previous experience taught Sebastian a lot could happen in those hours.

But Sebastian really, really wanted to just see a nice looking guy tonight. It had been so long since he had spoken, flirted or just done anything with a guy that he was starting to forget what it was like.

Sebastian felt an icy chill and heard the bitter howl of the December wind outside, and he just knew he had to get another handful of heaters and put them up. There was nothing worse in the entire world than having a wedding reception in the freezing cold.

That was never going to go down well.

But as Sebastian marched out of the reception area to get some little heaters from his van, he supposed the only thing worse than having a wedding in the cold, was going to a wedding completely alone.

How sad was that?

***

Bad boy Dylan simply couldn't believe he was at a wedding all alone and he was the only remotely attractive guy here.

He sat at the very back on a horribly cold hard pew of the large church. There were tens upon tens of people here sitting on the other pews and hanging onto every single silly word of the happy couple, but they were all women, old men or men that just weren't that attractive.

Dylan had to admit the bride did look nice in her long white flowing dress that made her look like some kind of angel, but that was Lilly through and through. She always had been a looker, and when Dylan was straight as they come he would have loved to do her one.

But that had changed a while ago.

Dylan wasn't exactly sure what Lilly had seen in Harrold. And come on, the name was just awful in itself, only posh idiots get called Harrold and the name certainly didn't belong with the little skinny peep.

Dylan still wasn't sure why Lilly had wanted him here, but he liked her and she was a dear friend. She was the first friend he told he was gay two years ago, and whilst she had been completely shocked. Because in her words, *you can't be gay Dyl. You slept with most the uni.*

Dylan still wasn't ashamed in the slightest that he had slept his way through university, and made sure all the women there had had fun and were okay about this only ever being a one-night stand. But Dylan realised he didn't want a relationship with women anymore.

In fact he wasn't that sure he ever actually did. Sometimes he just wondered if he tried to enjoy women because it was what his family wanted.

The playing of the church organ started up again and Dylan admitted to only himself that it was nice listening to the bride and the skinny little groom take their vows, promising to love each other no matter what and everything else that straight couples did.

There might have been a time when Dylan would have said that once with the only guy he had ever tried something with (that was actually before university) but that sweet little eighteen year old who was the same age as Dylan at the time, was just that.

Too sweet, but he was such a good guy.

Dylan sometimes wondered why he walked out after six weeks with such a wonderful, caring guy that clearly loved him. Sometimes he believed it was because Dylan could do better, other times it was because Dylan didn't want to settle down. But every so often, Dylan truly believed it was because he knew that guy (the name escaped him) could do so much better at the end of the today.

Because all Dylan was (and got repeatedly told was) he was nothing more than a sexual dinosaur that would never get a relationship and would die alone.

Everyone stood up as the bride and little skinny groom started to walk out of the church, and per Lilly's instructions the people sitting at the back were the last to leave.

Yet after Dylan had heard those two women tell him how he would die alone, he sort of lost all interest in women and relationships. And he honestly didn't know if he was a sexual dinosaur only interested in hook-ups before that comment, but he was now.

When Lilly had said there would be hot guys here, Dylan had been hoping he could pick up a group of them and they could all come back to his apartment. But judging by the awful lack of variety and attractiveness here, Dylan just knew that wasn't happening.

And it was only quarter-past five in the evening and he sadly couldn't leave until midnight. This was going to be an awful long and chase night for Dylan, not something he particularly enjoyed. Especially when his gay dating apps had been particularly active today, so many lost opportunities all because of a wedding.

With everyone leaving the church, Dylan followed the large group out into the biting cold church grounds towards a very large white tent.

As the group went towards it, Dylan was surprised how great the large Marple trees were looking with their bare branches, the layer of thick frost on the grass and the wide array of Christmas lights covering the reception tent and the church.

It was rather magical in a way.

Dylan heard the subtle playing of music coming from inside the reception tent and his stomach tensed. This wasn't his idea of fun and he just hoped that the tent was going to be a lot warmer than the stupid temperature out here.

But as Dylan walked into the large reception tent, he quickly decided if push comes to shove, Dylan was more than prepared to come here for a smoke and just leave the wedding.

He wasn't freezing his ass off for no reward. He was young, hot and fit he had things to do-

Fucking hell!

Dylan just stopped dead in his tracks as he spotted an outrageously hot sexy man standing at the head table quickly talking to Harrold and Lilly.

Dylan couldn't believe how amazing he looked in

his tight blue suit, shiny black shoes and bright blue eyes only amplified by his suit. The guy was hot as hell and very, very much someone Dylan wanted to do.

Yet at the same time, he actually felt drawn to just talk to the guy and see what he was doing here.

Dylan just knew that this guy was either the reason to stay or leave.

And Dylan really hoped he would stay.

***

Sebastian was flat out relieved to hear that the happy couple had had a wonderful wedding ceremony, and Sebastian would never ever admit it in public, but wow… Harrold seriously knew how to dress up smartly.

Unfortunately there had been a slight change to the menu to include tomato soup but Dylan had managed to make it special and delicious so that was one crisis averted.

Hopefully there would be no more.

As Sebastian left the happy couple to sit themselves down at the head table, the guests were sitting down at their carefully assigned round white tables and the little band at the back of the white reception tent played ever so slightly positive background music.

Just picking and designing this piece of music to create a constantly posh, sophisticated and positive atmosphere throughout the reception had been hard enough, but Sebastian listened to the quiet yet joyous piece of music. He was extremely pleased with what he had achieved.

With most of the delightful wedding guests seated, Sebastian started to walk towards the exit of the reception area so he could change into something slightly more comfortable so instead of looking like an up-tight wedding planner. He could hopefully look like just another wedding guest.

But judging by how all the hot men in the tent were sitting next to apparently beautiful (Sebastian couldn't tell) women. He really doubted he was going to meet, flirt and go home with anyone tonight.

"Excuse me," a deep manly voice said as Sebastian was about to leave the reception tent.

Sebastian turned around and… well.

Sebastian had never been expected to see such an outrageously hot man in all his life, and least not one he recognised and knew.

Even after dumping him years ago, Sebastian still recognised Dylan's amazing fit body in a very, very well-fitted black suit that highlighted all the right features right from his muscular arms to his chest and lower regions that still looked amazing.

He was hot.

Sebastian still loved Dylan's smooth handsome face that was so perfectly stunning that Sebastian doubted he would ever be dismissed as a model.

Sebastian felt his heart skip a few beats, his stomach filled with butterflies and he was just amazed he got to see his utterly stunning man again after all these years.

Granted, what from Sebastian had heard from friends and their friends over the years, Dylan was the type of guy it was best to avoid these days. He was a soulless, sexual dinosaur who didn't care about anyone.

Sebastian had never wanted to believe it, because whilst Dylan was apparently "straight" during their wonderful six weeks together. Sebastian had loved every moment of it because Dylan was hot, smart and just such a great person to be with.

But as Dylan stood in front of him, Sebastian stared at his beauty and there was just a vibe that Dylan was giving him. Maybe all the rumours were true and that Dylan was nothing more than a bad boy player nowadays.

Yet Sebastian at least wanted to talk to this sexy man.

"Didn't expect to see you again," Sebastian said.

Dylan's face was blank. Sebastian couldn't believe that Dylan didn't recognise him, had he really done so many guys in the past few years that he didn't remember a face anymore?

"I'm sorry do I know you?" Dylan asked.

Sebastian laughed. This was just unbelievable.

"Um yeah. I'm Sebastian. You know your six week relationship then you left me because you weren't gay,"

Dylan's mouth dropped. Even though Sebastian wanted to be so mad with him, he had to admit Dylan was just so cute.

"I'm... so sorry," he said.

Sebastian wanted to try and find something harsh, mocking or just awful in those words. But Dylan had said them with such sincerity that Sebastian had almost wanted to believe him.

Almost.

"Sorry about what?" Sebastian asked. "Leaving me? Abandoning me? Pretending to be straight?"

Dylan looked so ashamed of himself, and Sebastian wondered how many times had Dylan acted it out. And it was only now he was realising how annoyed he was with Dylan.

Sebastian had loved Dylan for so long that he supposed he just wanted to know was it ever real, or was it really just a worthless fling to Dylan.

Dylan looked to the ground. "I just wanted you to be with someone who deserved you. I'm not a good person. You've heard the rumours, you must have. I'm no good in relationships,"

Sebastian just smiled. That was such rubbish, Dylan had been so good, perfect and wonderful all those years ago. They had made each other laugh, cry and made passionate love together because they loved each other.

Dylan might have acted sometimes unsure of his sexuality, whether being gay was right and all the other rubbish young gay people have to figure out. But he was great.

But as Dylan just stood there with the sound of

wedding guests, the band and the food being served started Sebastian wasn't sure what to say.

So he just said what came to mind first.

Sebastian gently took Dylan's hand, and he seriously loved the amazing power, chemistry and feelings of love that flowed between them.

"You were great. I loved you. We had a great thing going and whatever happened I would have helped you through it. That's what boyfriends do,"

Dylan instantly recoiled at the mention of *boyfriends*. Like it was something to be ashamed of and like he was an abomination for even considering it.

Sebastian just shook his head, but even he couldn't deny he sensed or at least felt some kind of connection. Maybe it was love, a longing for Dylan or just another chance to see if what happened years ago could happen again (and hopefully for longer this time).

Maybe Dylan needed an ultimatum. Something Sebastian hated doing to people and clients, let alone a hot sexy man like Dylan.

"I'm going to get changed. Think about if you have anything you want to say to me. You have until I come back here. If you want to explain why you left me, then you have to say it then. Or don't say anything at all,"

To Sebastian's surprise Dylan furiously nodded like it was a serious thing that Dylan just had to complete and do because his life depended on it.

And Sebastian wasn't sure.

Maybe it did.

***

Dylan sat back down at his little round table filled with three happily laughing straight couples as they laughed and joked about him being the only single person there.

Two of the older couples were definitely slightly homophobic as they were saying that it was only right and by God's design that he was single, lonely and silly.

They were the silly ones.

Dylan loved the delightful smell of the delightfully creamy tomato soup with fresh hints of garlic and herbs that were coming from somewhere. Maybe there had been a change to the menu or something.

Whatever happened it smelt amazing.

Dylan just let the idiots joke around him as the soft and wonderful band played something soft as background music. It was rather wonderful in a way.

Since seeing Sebastian, and he was more than ashamed for not instantly recognising him, he had completely lost his sex drive and he was feeling things he hadn't felt for ages.

Sure, Dylan loved gay sex, having fun and snogging men. But he didn't want to do that now, he actually wanted to just leave the wedding and sit down and talk to Sebastian.

Out of all the different men and women he had been with over his lifetime, Sebastian was the only person who made him feel beautiful, perfect and honestly… loved.

Not sexually loved, but caringly loved. The way how married straight old couples talked about their love for one another and how they didn't need to have sex, constantly be with each other and talk to know that they loved each other.

Even when Dylan and Sebastian had been in opposite ends of their apartment doing their own thing. Dylan still knew that Sebastian loved him and that they were enjoying their time together.

And whenever they both went out in public, it just felt so natural for both of them. Dylan loved other people seeing he was lucky enough to be with Sebastian.

Until now he just hadn't realised that was how he felt.

But Sebastian was completely right to be mad at him. Dylan had been such an awful boyfriend to him, and he certainly didn't mean to pull away from him.

It was just that the word *boyfriend* for him had been used so strangely in past years. Dylan used to call his boyfriends the regular people he slept with, he hadn't felt in love since Sebastian.

And things were different now. Dylan was definitely gay, he didn't care that others knew and he just wanted Sebastian to be happy.

But what if history repeated itself?

"And I bet that fairy wedding planner had got to the wait staff. None of them were proper men like in my day," one of the older men at the table said.

Dylan watched the joking, laughing silly people sitting at his wedding table and what if he wanted to break up and run away from how he felt again?

He didn't want that for Sebastian. Sebastian was such a kind, sweet, cute guy that didn't deserve a liability like Dylan. Sebastian deserved someone that loved, treasured and just wanted to basically worship him (in a non-creepy way of course).

But that was how Dylan felt.

"And those benders could never feel the way I do about my beautiful wife. She was a vicar for over thirty years and she cured ten gays in her time. She is a saviour of humanity and the Satan's gay corruption," the elderly man said before he kissed his wife.

Dylan just rolled his eyes.

He had made up his mind and he was definitely going to be with Sebastian. He loved him. No matter what these dickheads were joking about.

Dylan stood up and everyone looked at him.

He looked at the elderly man with the former vicar wife.

"And you know what you homophobic dicks. I love men. Sure your bible doesn't permit it but I love what I love. And I damn well love that so-called fairy wedding planner. He is an amazing man. And if you have a problem with me and him, then just go fuck yourself!"

Dylan spun around.

Sebastian was standing there smiling.

Dylan grabbed him and left.

***

Of all the things that Sebastian had been expecting for Dylan to say it certainly hadn't been that.

As they both walked through the biting bitter cold of the church grounds with the stunning bare maple trees, frosted grass and the little white reception tent behind them. Sebastian just walked with wonderful Dylan arm in arm.

Sebastian seriously loved the amazing feeling of Dylan's hard warm body against his.

The air was wonderfully crisp, fresh and cold, just perfect for a little romantic walk through the grounds of a place that hated them.

In all honesty Sebastian had been expecting Dylan to say that he wasn't interested, he never wanted a relationship and that he was only interested in a quick shag.

But as Sebastian hugged Dylan, there was just something so right about tonight, being with him and their unspoken love between them. And Sebastian definitely knew that all the rumours were true about Dylan.

Yet somehow the rumours were all false now.

For an uncaring sexual dinosaur never would have cared about Sebastian enough to say what he did or take a wonderfully relaxing walk in the pitch darkness with him. Dylan was definitely after something a lot deeper, and Sebastian wanted that too.

In fact he seriously wanted it.

"I never meant to hurt you. I just wanted to figure myself out and... some people just said something that changed my perspective," Dylan said.

"And turned you into a dinosaur like the rumours said?"

Dylan said looking to the floor.

Sebastian stopped them both and lifted up Dylan's head with his finger, so that he stared into Dylan's wonderfully soft eyes.

"I don't care about the past. I care about the future," Sebastian said.

Dylan gave him such a schoolboy smile and Sebastian felt it too. Sebastian felt like he had all those years ago and all their past feelings of attraction, love and longing to be together was back.

Sebastian wanted to love and treasure and be with Dylan until they both died. And in a way it was only fitting they were at the end where it was literally til death did them part.

And one of Sebastian's favourite things about Dylan and him was that they were almost always on the same wave length, and that only made Dylan more cute.

If such a thing was possible.

"We're really doing this then, aren't we?" Dylan said smiling.

Sebastian looked back at the reception tent.

Harrold and Lilly were hugging and looking at them, then Sebastian noticed that those homophobic idiots were moaning as they had been kicked out of the wedding.

"I think our friends want us back," Sebastian said.

Dylan smiled and held out his hand in front of him.

"I want you if you'll have me back," Dylan said.

Sebastian wrapped his hand round Dylan's wonderfully soft warm one as they walked back towards the reception tent, and Sebastian just instantly knew that there was no place or person he would rather have at his side than Dylan.

Sure their romance might have stopped and started over the years, but now Sebastian just knew that Dylan wanted to be with him forever.

And Sebastian was the same.

After all they were at a wonderful winter wedding. And that only meant one thing.

Til death does them part.

And Sebastian had no problems with that.

FIREWORKS, NEW YEAR, LOVE

Grayson Brown had always absolutely loved New Years' eve with the clubbing, partying and fireworks that made him feel so happy and excited about the amazing new year ahead of him.

And after all the rubbish he had had to deal with in the past year with his brother, work and some drama with old long gone friends, Grayson was seriously looking forward to the fun of a new years party!

Grayson stood in his large spacious bedroom with posh shirts, trousers and more covering his double bed behind him whilst he stood in front of a mirror trying to decide what to wear tonight.

The large warm lights in his bedroom made sure Grayson could see himself and his lean body in the mirror, but he partly didn't like how bright his bedroom lights were, they made him feel so vain. Whereas in all honesty he didn't particularly care how he looked.

As long as he was attractive for guys he didn't really care too much.

Grayson was glad no one else was with himself in his room was they would probably be choked out of all his earthy, flowery and spicy aftershaves that he had tried on for tonight. They all combined in the air to create a wonderful but extremely strong concoction that Grayson sort of knew would put off men rather than attract them.

He wasn't even sure why he was trying so hard. Grayson was only going to a new years eve party at one of his best friend's friend's house, and Grayson's best friend Cora had promised there would be other gay guys there too.

At first that had hardly won Grayson over because he wasn't all about meeting other gays, having hook-ups and doing all that casual sex thing of the gay community. Instead he wanted relationships, fun and love.

Something he seriously wasn't getting at the moment. Grayson had tried online dating, finding gay guys at university a few years ago and dating a few people at work.

Nothing had worked.

So Grayson was hardly surprised he eventually caved when Cora kept asking him out of love and not wanting to see him without a boyfriend for too long. She really was a great friend like that.

The sound of Cora's high heels pounding downstairs made Grayson wonder even more about what to wear tonight. Cora had gotten here earlier, Grayson had cooked them a quick vegan chicken coconut curry and she had gotten ready quickly enough.

Grayson had no idea how Cora, the woman that took two hours to get ready for any party, had managed to get ready before him.

After looking at a tight sexy white shirt in the mirror Grayson just wasn't sure, so he fell onto his bed and just took a deep breath of the aftershave scented air.

Why was this so hard?

Grayson was normally a wonderfully calm organised guy who knew exactly who and what he wanted in life. At work he knew he wanted to get promoted to Manager and he knew he wanted his friend Harry there to be his boyfriend.

But it quickly turned out that Harry was a snake in the grass and tried to embarrass Grayson in front of everyone. The dickhead.

Grayson heard Cora's high heels pound up the stairs and Grayson knew he just had to decide quickly because otherwise Cora would choose for him.

And whilst Cora was an amazing friend, there was a very, very good reason why she was single and unable to get boys. She dressed… interestingly to say the least and even if Grayson was straight. He absolutely knew for a fact he would never ever want to sleep with Cora.

A few moments later Cora opened Grayson's

bedroom door, sneezed at the heavy scent of aftershave and just smiled at him.

Grayson had to admit tonight she looked a lot better in her little black dress, 6-inch heels (that she would definitely fall over in at some point) and her boobs that was normally on full show were sensibly hidden in her dress.

Grayson was more than relieved about that because the last thing he wanted was to have protected Cora against guys who were only interested in her female parts. Grayson had had to do that too many times before.

Some guys were just sexual monsters.

"Jeans, white shirt, come on," Cora said smiling.

Grayson stood and looked at the tight white shirt he had been looking at only moments ago. It was nice and it had helped him… definitely know he was gay before, so it might be a lucky shirt in a way.

Grayson quickly threw on the white shirt, a pair of skin tight black jeans and some boots.

"Nice," Cora said with an evil grin. "Oh believe me, my friend's friends will like you,"

Grayson didn't know how to take that. He was starting to feel like this was less of a new years eve party and more of a blind date or something a lot more sexual.

Grayson just didn't know what option he wanted as they both rushed out the door.

***

Former British Army Soldier Ethan Painter hated

new years eve with a passion, he also hated Bonfire night on the 5th November for the exact same reason.

He hated fireworks.

Where most people saw fireworks as wonderful flashes of colour organised into breathtaking displays of skill, power and colour. Ethan only saw weapons like flashed like IEDs and explosives that sounded like his friends being ripped apart in the middle east.

Even after five years out of the army Ethan still hated New Years Eve, and no one ever seemed to try and understand him. Ethan had only politely asked his neighbours either side of his little house, please don't have fireworks. But they both laughed at him and told him to man up.

Ethan wanted to shout and moan at them and tell them the definition of *manning up* and all that crap. He would love to see what they would do if their armoured vehicle had been blown off the road and ripped open with enemy soldiers coming in all directions.

Ethan knew exactly what that was like because all his fellow soldiers, ten of them in total, had been killed. Leaving Ethan to defend himself until help arrived.

All Ethan had gotten for his bravery and surviving for three long hours was a medal, a discharge and some kind of government handout. In all fairness, Ethan knew it was exactly the excuse his commanding officer had wanted. He always said, *letting gays into the army was the biggest mistake ever. Better to let them all go.*

As Ethan sat on a large swinging chair in his small garden with carefully maintained rose beds, vegetable patch and some oak trees lining the garden. Ethan felt his stomach grow more and more tense as the sun was setting, the cold was dropping and soon it would all begin.

Ethan had to be inside when the evil fireworks started. He would try to be in bed when the explosions started but he knew that was useless. He would be woken up and Ethan's mind would fill with the scenes of explosions back in the warzone.

Ethan hated new Year's eve.

As much as Ethan tried to reach out to the military veteran services for support and guidance and other veterans he knew. Nothing seemed to help and no one in Ethan's new job as a security consultant seemed to remotely care about his fears of fireworks.

And after a while the veteran support services blocked his calls.

No one cared about him.

That was probably one of the few things he hated about the military and the government. They were all happy and nice when you were fighting, suffering and dying for them. But the second you weren't, you were just another pleb on the street as far as they were concerned.

Ethan just focused on the slight chill of his skin, the wonderful smell of a neighbour's barbeque and the smoke, sausages and burgers scents that were coming from that. He just needed to live in the moment.

After a few moments, Ethan realised that it was a bit too cold to stay out here any longer so he went inside his house, through the large perfectly clean dining room with its large table, chairs and cabinets filled with photos of long dead friends and medals.

And Ethan went straight into his little kitchen with its bright white cabinets, large six hob stove and a very tall white kitchen that stood as straight as a soldier in the corner.

If Ethan was going to suffer tonight then he would much rather be a little tipsy and maybe drunk and just maybe that would stop the worse of the emotional pain he was in.

Ethan opened up his icy cold fridge and frowned as he looked in the side shelves and realised he was completely out of alcohol. Granted he probably never had some in the first place considering he ever so rarely drank, but Ethan was hopeful that his last boyfriend about six months ago had bought some for himself.

But that insensitive jerk had probably taken them all for himself when he left.

Ethan felt his heart speed up as he realised he was going to have to go out or suffer completely tonight.

Ethan couldn't survive another year of constant explosions and reliving those horrific memories constantly. And then you had all the idiots who launched their fireworks at one, two and later in the early morning.

No! Ethan couldn't do that again.

Ethan took a long deep breath of the cold refrigerated air and knew he was going to have to go out and get some alcohol.

There was a store a few blocks away.

And Ethan just hoped beyond hope that no idiot would set off a firework early.

***

Grayson and Cora laughed as she told him about her latest failed sexual conquest at a local bar the other night. Grayson couldn't believe how badly that had gone and how badly she had embarrassed herself with her entire dress catching on a bar stool and ripping off.

Cora seemed perfectly okay about it and like it was just part of life. That was seriously something Grayson loved about her, she was always in control and perfectly so.

Grayson kept laughing as the two of them went into a little corner shop with its rows upon rows of neatly organised food, drinks and other little products that people might need.

The only reason they were in there was because Cora wanted to buy some alcohol for the party, and she really, really wanted Grayson to buy some adult protection.

Grayson still didn't know what to make of this party she was taking him to, because it was starting to sound less and less innocent by the second, but Grayson couldn't deny he wasn't looking forward to it all.

Yet as Grayson started to walk down a little aisle with Cora that was filled with more black wine bottles than Grayson had ever seen before, Grayson's stomach filled with butterflies at the idea of the party being great fun. It had been far too long since he had that kind of fun.

As Cora mumbled to herself about the wine choices, Grayson just flat out didn't understand what was so special about the different wines. They were all just black bottles with different coloured labels to him.

Granted there were some bottles with pretty pink wine or *rosa* on the bottom shelf, but Grayson wasn't going to buy anything. He doubted he would make the right decision and Cora was definitely more of the wine expert than he was.

As Cora continued to mumble and moan to herself, Grayson heard the bell to the little store open and he turned to see out of pure curiosity who had walked into the store.

Holy fuck!

Grayson's mouth dropped at the stunning looking guy walking into the little store with his broad shoulders, clearly muscular body with a very clear six pack and biceps and more under his thick coat.

And that face. Grayson was completely seduced by the guy's hot stunning face that was framed so perfectly by the rest of his body, and there was something slightly familiar about him.

Well not him per se. But Grayson certainly recognised the posture, haircut and carefully scanning of the environment from when his older brother and sister had enlisted and trained in the army. Grayson never wanted to experience or think or mention what his brother went through or did ever again.

Grayson had wanted to join too, but given how homophobic the people in charge were (who had all had gay sex) Grayson just didn't see the point.

If Grayson wanted to work in a homophobic environment, there were definitely a lot better paying jobs than the army.

"Grayson!" Cora shouted in his ear.

Grayson jumped. "What?"

"Are you listening to me?" Cora asked sharply.

Grayson shook his head and his attention snapped back onto the absolutely stunning man walking down towards him. Grayson loved seeing how confident the man was as he walked towards them.

That was just flat out sexy.

The man didn't look at Grayson or Cora as he glided past them and started looking at the wine.

Grayson went right up to Cora's ear. "Give me some posh wine fact,"

Cora didn't understand. Grayson gestured to the stunning guy.

"He's straight babe. Men like him always are,"

Cora said, moving closer to the man.

Grayson just watched as Cora flirted, smiled and started talking to the man. Then the stunning guy kindly smiled and said that he wasn't interested in women and that he hoped she had a good night.

Cora walked past frowning. It took everything Grayson had not to start wetting himself laughing.

A firework went off outside.

Grayson could never understand the idiots that decided to set off their fireworks this early in the evening.

Wine bottles smashed to the ground.

"Help!" the stunning man shouted.

Grayson spun around. The stunning man looked so scared, panicked and frightened. His eyes were scanning the store, he acted like there was a rifle in his hands.

Grayson had to help him.

"What's going on!" the male owner shouted as he came down the aisle.

Grayson waved him away.

The stunning man jumped. Smashing more bottles.

Grayson slowly lowered himself onto his knees and held out his arms to the stunning man.

"Hey there," Grayson said slowly. "I'm Grayson. What's your name?"

The stunning man backed away. His eyes wide and scared of Grayson.

Grayson slowly edged closer.

"You're safe soldier. The enemy are gone. You made it," Grayson said.

The man seemed to relax just a bit more. Grayson continued to edge forward.

Until Grayson could jump the stunning man and hug him tight.

The stunning man struggled a little bit but Grayson started to do long deep breaths and after a few moments the soldier copied his breathing and relaxed.

Grayson couldn't deny how amazing the stunning man's hard body felt against his, and if the man hadn't just had an attack of something. Grayson would probably try to kiss him.

To Grayson's surprise the stunning man didn't try to push him away, the man simply smiled and moved his head so he could probably get a better look at Grayson.

The stunning man looked like he wanted to say something but he looked too shocked to do it. Grayson had a few inappropriate things he wanted to say, but he felt his hands get sweaty and clammy and there was something a lot more useful he could do.

"Let me help you home," Grayson said.

The stunning man slowly nodded.

As Grayson helped him up, Cora was being her typically amazing self and was paying for all the damaged bottles, and she just smiled at him.

"I'll pay you back?" Grayson asked as the two men left the store.

"I know you will!" Cora shouted with a massive grin.

***

As Ethan was helped into his large spacious living room with two large white sofas, a large coffee table in front of them and a massive home entertainment system, he just couldn't believe how embarrassed he was.

The sexy man who had helped Ethan home gently helped him onto one of the sofas and thankfully he just sat next to Ethan.

Ethan loved how the smaller sexy man felt against him. Ethan had loved how the man carefully and caringly held him, supported him and Ethan just flat out loved the sheer chemistry that flowed through them.

Ethan had never met such a gorgeous cute man in all his life, and that included some of the guys in the military with bodies like Greek Gods. Ethan seriously loved the man's small lean frame, tight jeans and very tight white shirt.

This sexy man was just beautiful.

And the smell of his earthy aftershave was so overwhelming but Ethan really loved it.

As Ethan stared at the cute man sitting next to him, he couldn't believe how compassionate and kind he had been. Most people during his panic attacks or semi-PTSD episodes didn't know how to react and they just left him.

But this sexy man didn't.

In fact he had known exactly how to take control of the situation, calm him down and protect him. Also people normally acted like he was the danger and not the awful fireworks that caused in.

But again this sexy man knew that Ethan wasn't the real danger. And that was just amazing to him.

Clearly the sexy man's lack of muscles, small frame and youthfulness (even though he was probably the same age as Ethan) meant he had never been in the military. So Ethan couldn't understand how this amazing man knew what to do?

Then Ethan realised even more that the sexy man hadn't revealed his name. On the short walk back here the sexy man had focused completely on distracting Ethan from the outside world and gotten him focused on the questions about his life that the man was asking.

The sexy man was amazing.

"Um," Ethan said. "Thanks for that. What's ya name?"

The sexy man smiled and Ethan wondered if he was about to have a heart attack. The sexy man's smile was simply out of this world.

"I'm Grayson and your welcome," Grayson said, leaning closer to him.

Ethan seriously wanted Grayson to hold him again but Grayson seemed to be sitting just far enough away to make that impossible.

"How did you know how to do that?" Ethan asked.

Grayson frowned a little. Ethan worried that he had overstepped the mark, he should have just been grateful that Grayson knew what to do.

Grayson must have picked up on Ethan's annoyance at himself as he grabbed his again. Again Ethan utterly loved the electricity shooting between them.

"My brother and sister," Grayson said. "They both served. My sister did three tours in the middle east, she came back fine. My brother..."

Ethan gently rubbed Grayson's hand.

"My brother wasn't very okay. He had severe PTSD. The doctors didn't do anything for months so my brother kept breaking down, screaming in the middle of the night and..."

Ethan knew exactly what he was about to say. He had seen the look in Grayson's eyes way too many times not to know that his brother was dead, and he never even thought or talked about it.

"When?" Ethan carefully asked.

"Last year. He apparently had a breakdown in the middle of a road, a car backfired and another car didn't stop in time," Grayson said.

Ethan pulled him close and kissed the sexy beautiful man on the head.

"I'm sorry," Ethan said, giving him another kiss.

"Don't be. I saved you. That... almost enough for me,"

Ethan smiled at that comment and felt his wayward parts spring to life. Clearly Grayson having him wasn't enough for him either.

Grayson slowly pulled his face out of Ethan's chest and he looked into Ethan's eyes. Ethan loved staring into Grayson's bright wonderful eyes and he saw something he hadn't seen for ages.

Ethan felt himself staring at a beautiful man who was being vulnerable for the first time in ages. And that's when Ethan realised the real Grayson was a lot more sensitive, warm and intimate than most people believed.

He had been looking at Grayson earlier in the little store when he was standing there with his friend. Grayson had looked so confident but it looked forced and it was probably part of an act that was just so apart of him now. That even he didn't realise that he was acting.

Ethan had seen more than enemy and friendly soldiers have to do it over the years. It was easy for Ethan now to know if someone was confident or not.

Then there was Grayson talking about all the sex and hot guys and what not at this party he was meant to be doing too on the walk back here.

But Ethan could just tell he didn't really want to go to that and have tons of pointless sex, because Ethan was starting to realise all that Grayson really wanted was connection, love and a relationship.

Maybe just a relationship of understanding, shared experience and knowing what each other went through. But still Grayson wanted a true relationship.

And Ethan wanted to give it to him.

"What would make this enough for you?" Ethan asked, loving the sense of connection he was feeling.

Grayson looked at the clock and Ethan noticed it was only nine o'clock at night. Plenty of time before the new year and what it would bring.

"Let me stay til midnight. I'll protect you," Grayson said.

Ethan was about to say yes then stopped. Not because he didn't want Grayson here, he really did, but he was utterly surprised that he didn't sound condescending, negative or judgmental about Ethan struggling with midnight fireworks.

Grayson was clearly a man who understood literally all of this and wanted to help Ethan out of care or compassion or hopefully love.

Ethan had never ever had someone do that for him before.

Ethan just kissed Grayson.

That was the only answer Ethan wanted to give.

***

Over the course of the next three hours, Grayson had wiped away so many tears, his stomach was hurting from laughing so much and his heart was as light as a feather in love. He had learnt so much about what his brother must have gone through and Grayson shared tons of little techniques and tips for helping Ethan.

Now as it approached midnight, Grayson sat with Ethan on a black swinging chair in his wonderful garden with roses, a vegetable patch and more great plants that Grayson was sure looked amazing in the summer.

The air was biting cold with hints of smoke, mulled wine and love that made Grayson wrap his arms round Ethan's stunning body even more.

And life really felt perfect as the two sat there waiting for all the fireworks to kick off.

For the first time since his brother had died, Grayson had actually thought about him, his family and how the death had affected all of them. Ethan was definitely right about him wanting to protect himself too much, and in the space of a few hours, Grayson had told more to Ethan than he had to anyone. Even Cora.

It surprised Grayson that he didn't feel ashamed in the slightest. Cora might have been an amazing friend but the wounds of his brother and everything surrounding the death had been such a buried blacked out secret that Grayson didn't want to tell anyone.

But somehow this hot sexy man had borrowed it out of him, and Grayson felt amazing and the lightest he had in years.

"Thank you," Grayson said kissing the man he honestly loved.

Ethan just smiled. It was such a happy schoolboy grin that Grayson had never seen anyone give him before.

It felt amazing to have someone look at him like that.

"No. Thank you, Ethan said. "You saved me,"

Grayson didn't agree with that entirely. He had only helped, but maybe in some way they had both saved each other. Grayson had saved Ethan from suffering tonight, and hot sexy Ethan had definitely saved Grayson from the blacked out pain of the past year.

"We saved each other," Grayson said, kissing the love of his life as the fireworks started.

Massive bright red, blue and green fireworks screamed into the sky.

But as Grayson and Ethan just held each other in their arms, Grayson noticed that Ethan wasn't reacting strongly or violently or panicked. He was shaking slightly but he was okay.

Maybe Grayson had saved him after all.

And Grayson just knew whatever the wonderful new year bought, they would do it and handle it and love it together because they were no longer two broken people each with their own secrets.

They were now together, two broken pieces put together to make a very loving and sexy whole that would last til the end of days.

And Grayson was more than fine with that.

GET YOUR FREE AND EXCLUSIVE SHORT STORY NOW! LEARN ABOUT NEMESIO'S PAST!

https://www.subscribepage.com/fireheart

Keep up to date with exclusive deals on Connor Whiteley's Books, as well as the latest news about new releases and so much more!

Sign up for the Grab a Book and Chill Monthly newsletter, and you'll get one **FREE** ebook just for signing up: Agents of The Emperor Collection.

Sign Up Now!

https://dl.bookfunnel.com/f4p5xkprbk

https://www.subscribepage.com/psychologyboxset

About the author:

Connor Whiteley is the author of over 60 books in the sci-fi fantasy, nonfiction psychology and books for writer's genre and he is a Human Branding Speaker and Consultant.

He is a passionate warhammer 40,000 reader, psychology student and author.

Who narrates his own audiobooks and he hosts The Psychology World Podcast.

All whilst studying Psychology at the University of Kent, England.

Also, he was a former Explorer Scout where he gave a speech to the Maltese President in August 2018 and he attended Prince Charles' 70th Birthday Party at Buckingham Palace in May 2018.

Plus, he is a self-confessed coffee lover!

OTHER SHORT STORIES BY CONNOR WHITELEY

<u>Gay Romance Short Stories:</u>
Round The Parks and Beyond
Heart Around the Stones
Memorable Night
Love in Halls
The One That Got Away
Gay Romance Collection
Love In The Ingreditents
Party, Love, Christmas
Love In The Wait
Gay, Love, Heir
Wedding, Guests and Love
Gay Romance Collection Volume 2

<u>Mystery Short Stories:</u>
A Smokey Way To Go
A Spicy Way To GO
A Marketing Way To Go
A Missing Way To Go
A Showering Way To Go
Poison In The Candy Cane
Christmas Innocence
You Better Watch Out
Christmas Theft
Trouble In Christmas
Smell of The Lake
Problem In A Car
Theft, Past and Team
Embezzler In The Room

A Strange Way To Go
A Horrible Way To Go
Ann Awful Way To Go
An Old Way To Go
A Fishy Way To Go
A Pointy Way To Go
A High Way To Go
A Fiery Way To Go
A Glassy Way To Go
A Chocolatey Way To Go
Kendra Detective Mystery Collection Volume 1
Kendra Detective Mystery Collection Volume 2
Stealing A Chance At Freedom
Glassblowing and Death
Theft of Independence
Cookie Thief
Marble Thief
Book Thief
Art Thief
Mated At The Morgue
The Big Five Whoopee Moments
Stealing An Election
Mystery Short Story Collection Volume 1
Mystery Short Story Collection Volume 2

GAY SWEET ROMANCE COLLECTION

<u>Science Fiction Short Stories:</u>
Gummy Bear Detective
The Candy Detective
What Candies Fear
The Blurred Image
Shattered Legions
The First Rememberer
Life of A Rememberer
System of Wonder
Lifesaver
Remarkable Way She Died
The Interrogation of Annabella Stormic
Blade of The Emperor
Arbiter's Truth
Computation of Battle
Old One's Wrath
Puppets and Masters
Ship of Plague
Interrogation
Edge of Failure
One Way Choice
Acceptable Losses
Balance of Power
Good Idea At The Time
Escape Plan
Escape In The Hesitation
Inspiration In Need
Singing Warriors
Knowledge is Power
Killer of Polluters

Climate of Death
The Family Mailing Affair
Defining Criminality
The Martian Affair
A Cheating Affair
The Little Café Affair
Mountain of Death
Prisoner's Fight
Claws of Death
Bitter Air
Honey Hunt
Blade On A Train

<u>Fantasy Short Stories:</u>
City of Snow
City of Light
City of Vengeance
Dragons, Goats and Kingdom
Smog The Pathetic Dragon
Don't Go In The Shed
The Tomato Saver
The Remarkable Way She Died
The Bloodied Rose
Asmodia's Wrath
Heart of A Killer
Emissary of Blood
Dragon Coins
Dragon Tea
Dragon Rider
Sacrifice of the Soul

GAY SWEET ROMANCE COLLECTION

Heart of The Flesheater
Heart of The Regent
Heart of The Standing
Feline of The Lost
Heart of The Story
City of Fire
Awaiting Death

Other books by Connor Whiteley:

Bettie English Private Eye Series
A Very Private Woman
The Russian Case
A Very Urgent Matter
A Case Most Personal
Trains, Scots and Private Eyes
The Federation Protects

The Fireheart Fantasy Series
Heart of Fire
Heart of Lies
Heart of Prophecy
Heart of Bones
Heart of Fate

City of Assassins (Urban Fantasy)
City of Death
City of Marytrs
City of Pleasure
City of Power

Agents of The Emperor
Return of The Ancient Ones
Vigilance
Angels of Fire
Kingmaker

GAY SWEET ROMANCE COLLECTION

<u>The Garro Series- Fantasy/Sci-fi</u>
GARRO: GALAXY'S END
GARRO: RISE OF THE ORDER
GARRO: END TIMES
GARRO: SHORT STORIES
GARRO: COLLECTION
GARRO: HERESY
GARRO: FAITHLESS
GARRO: DESTROYER OF WORLDS
GARRO: COLLECTIONS BOOK 4-6
GARRO: MISTRESS OF BLOOD
GARRO: BEACON OF HOPE
GARRO: END OF DAYS

<u>Winter Series- Fantasy Trilogy Books</u>
WINTER'S COMING
WINTER'S HUNT
WINTER'S REVENGE
WINTER'S DISSENSION

<u>Miscellaneous:</u>
RETURN
FREEDOM
SALVATION
Reflection of Mount Flame
The Masked One
The Great Deer

All books in 'An Introductory Series':

BIOLOGICAL PSYCHOLOGY 3RD EDITION
COGNITIVE PSYCHOLOGY THIRD EDITION
SOCIAL PSYCHOLOGY- 3RD EDITION
ABNORMAL PSYCHOLOGY 3RD EDITION
PSYCHOLOGY OF RELATIONSHIPS- 3RD EDITION
DEVELOPMENTAL PSYCHOLOGY 3RD EDITION
HEALTH PSYCHOLOGY
RESEARCH IN PSYCHOLOGY
A GUIDE TO MENTAL HEALTH AND TREATMENT AROUND THE WORLD- A GLOBAL LOOK AT DEPRESSION
FORENSIC PSYCHOLOGY
THE FORENSIC PSYCHOLOGY OF THEFT, BURGLARY AND OTHER CRIMES AGAINST PROPERTY
CRIMINAL PROFILING: A FORENSIC PSYCHOLOGY GUIDE TO FBI PROFILING AND GEOGRAPHICAL AND STATISTICAL PROFILING.
CLINICAL PSYCHOLOGY
FORMULATION IN PSYCHOTHERAPY
PERSONALITY PSYCHOLOGY AND INDIVIDUAL DIFFERENCES
CLINICAL PSYCHOLOGY REFLECTIONS VOLUME 1
CLINICAL PSYCHOLOGY REFLECTIONS VOLUME 2

GAY SWEET ROMANCE COLLECTION

CULT PSYCHOLOGY
Police Psychology

A Psychology Student's Guide To University
How Does University Work?
A Student's Guide To University And Learning
University Mental Health and Mindset

Companion guides:
BIOLOGICAL PSYCHOLOGY 2ND EDITION WORKBOOK
COGNITIVE PSYCHOLOGY 2ND EDITION WORKBOOK
SOCIOCULTURAL PSYCHOLOGY 2ND EDITION WORKBOOK
ABNORMAL PSYCHOLOGY 2ND EDITION WORKBOOK
PSYCHOLOGY OF HUMAN RELATIONSHIPS 2ND EDITION WORKBOOK
HEALTH PSYCHOLOGY WORKBOOK
FORENSIC PSYCHOLOGY WORKBOOK

Audiobooks by Connor Whiteley:
BIOLOGICAL PSYCHOLOGY
COGNITIVE PSYCHOLOGY
SOCIOCULTURAL PSYCHOLOGY
ABNORMAL PSYCHOLOGY
PSYCHOLOGY OF HUMAN RELATIONSHIPS
HEALTH PSYCHOLOGY

DEVELOPMENTAL PSYCHOLOGY
RESEARCH IN PSYCHOLOGY
FORENSIC PSYCHOLOGY
GARRO: GALAXY'S END
GARRO: RISE OF THE ORDER
GARRO: SHORT STORIES
GARRO: END TIMES
GARRO: COLLECTION
GARRO: HERESY
GARRO: FAITHLESS
GARRO: DESTROYER OF WORLDS
GARRO: COLLECTION BOOKS 4-6
GARRO: COLLECTION BOOKS 1-6

Business books:
TIME MANAGEMENT: A GUIDE FOR STUDENTS AND WORKERS
LEADERSHIP: WHAT MAKES A GOOD LEADER? A GUIDE FOR STUDENTS AND WORKERS.
BUSINESS SKILLS: HOW TO SURVIVE THE BUSINESS WORLD? A GUIDE FOR STUDENTS, EMPLOYEES AND EMPLOYERS.
BUSINESS COLLECTION

GET YOUR FREE BOOK AT:
WWW.CONNORWHITELEY.NET

www.ingramcontent.com/pod-product-compliance
Lightning Source LLC
LaVergne TN
LVHW012104070526
838202LV00056B/5617